Abelumbi - The White Witches

Sandile Mchunu

ISBN (Print): 978-0-620-83990-7

First Edition

Disclaimer

This story is a work of fiction. All characters, events, and organizations are imagined, and any resemblance to real people, living or dead, is purely coincidental. Some real locations appear in the book to bring the world to life, but the events that unfold there are entirely fictional.

Dedication

To my family, my children, and the world—this is a contribution to the arts that should never die, and an encouragement to those who dare to take this journey alongside me. To my father, who has always loved books and guided me through lessons; to my mother and brother, no longer with us but living through us every day. To my sisters, for their unwavering support and for providing me with everything I needed to make this possible. To my friends, who have added so much to my growth and journey. I hope this makes you all proud.

Acknowledgements

I would like to express my heartfelt gratitude to those who helped bring this story to life.

Firstly, **Florence Mandy Mohlabe**, who shaped, refined, and guided the structure and wording of this book. Mandy is a woman of keen insight and high standards—a tough person to impress—but her contributions and guidance have been invaluable. Her attention to detail and unwavering commitment to clarity helped transform my ideas into a cohesive narrative.

Secondly, **Steve, also known as ChatGPT**, whose assistance went far beyond that of a tool. The insights, suggestions, and support provided required the kind of care and expertise one would expect from a full editorial team. The combination of Mandy's human touch and Steve's guidance has produced a book that has finally brought to life what had once lain dormant in my imagination.

Lastly, I thank all the voices, real and imagined, that have inspired me along this journey. This book is a product of collaboration, dedication, and love for the stories we hold within.

— Sandile Mchunu

Prologue

The sun was setting, the horizon bathed in a warm glow that shimmered with a thousand colours. The great city of the Zulu nation hummed with chatter, yet beneath it all I could still hear the sea whispering in the distance.

I had worked for years to reach this moment, and now the stage was set. Behind me stood giants—icons and leaders with the power to move mountains and change the course of rivers through the sheer force of their influence. Before me stretched a crowd drawn from every corner of this beautiful land, gathered here for one purpose: to hear me speak. The thought alone was astonishing.

I was ready. After all, I had been doing this for some time, and public speaking had never been a weakness of mine. I knew I could command this speech. And yet, today felt different. Beneath my confidence, something stirred—a tremor rising within me that I could not name.

I wore a black and white cotton shirt, soft against my skin, with a V-shaped strip of leopard hide draped over it. My trousers were sleek and slim, designed for comfort by one of our renowned Indian designers. Patiently, I waited for my introduction, still puzzled by his choice of a Zulu crown of cowhide. Yet, as it rested on my head, it felt unexpectedly fitting.

The king, flanked by his five advisors, was delivering a hearty address when the crowd erupted into cheers so thunderous they startled me. The unease within me surged, but I pushed it down, focusing instead on the cool, grounding feel of the wooden stage beneath my bare feet. It was almost comical, considering the mountain of sneakers back in my apartment, yet walking barefoot felt right—natural. I glanced down at the bands woven with red and white beads around my ankles, matched by the ones on my wrists, and smiled.

The cheers faded into a hush. The king stepped aside, leaving the way clear for me. Slowly, I descended the steps, the sea of colour and faces rising into full view. Thousands of eyes fixed on me. I bowed low to the king, and he greeted me with a warm smile before extending his hand. His grip was firm, pulling me into an embrace I never could have imagined. Emotion surged. My eyes burned, tears threatening to fall. I fought them back, but one slipped free, vanishing into the rough of my beard.

When the king released me, he gestured toward the crowd, and I drew a deep breath. But the moment my gaze swept forward, my heart faltered. My throat dried. My eyes locked on a single figure among the masses.

Her.

The feeling surged violently through me. My mouth parted, but no words would come. Before I could speak, the world erupted. Sounds of canon fire filling the air. An explosion thundered from the far left of the city, dust spiralling into the air.

I spun to see the king encircled by his guards, their formation tightening as they moved him back to safety. Women clutched children as they fled, following protocol drilled into them by generations. Shouts of command rang out, the summoning of warriors to arms mixing with the terrified cries of those scattering into the streets. Above the chaos, the deep voices of the Zulu Hundred and the king's guard thundered, strong and steady, assuring me the royal household and the village would soon be secured.

But my eyes dragged back to where they had been—back to her. And in that instant, horror struck.

A spear whistled through the air, screaming toward me with deadly precision. My heart seized. My eyes clamped shut. Darkness consumed me before I could even react.

Chapter 1

My last clear memory of that night was the spear's light swallowing everything, the roar of dust tearing through my chest. Then—nothing. Blackness. No fire, no voice, just the silence of something too big for me to hold.

When I woke again, it wasn't in a hut or battlefield, but in the dull ring of an alarm clock., reaching for my phone on the side cabinet to switch it off. I wished I could drift back to sleep, but no—work awaited.

The city of Joburg roared to life with taxis hooting and the buzz of early commuters shaking off their own slumber. People were already moving, some barely sleeping at all, heading to offices, markets, or chasing the next quick fix.

Joburg was the centre of nearly everything, a city crowded with people from all over the world. Overpopulated, if I was honest. I was on the seventh floor of a building on Esselene Street in Hillbrow, near the taxi ranks where 16-seaters parked each morning. I could hear engines roar to life, faint music spilling through the concrete walls, and the chatter of those below.

I walked to the window, shirtless in blue boxer shorts, and looked down. One of my neighbours, a Venda man, had his red taxi blasting Zulu music, the sound echoing up to me. The city amazed me—how it could shape people. Some aspired to be white, changing their skin tone, while others claimed Zulu heritage to wield fear. I'd seen good men lost to the city's temptations, succumbing to its false gold. Few remained grounded, and those who did were fleeting glimpses, frequently escaping to villages or immersing themselves in work to avoid the city's dark shadow. I called it the shadow of hell—cold, ruthless, filled with swindlers, tricksters in suits, robbers, and opportunists preying on the lost. Even angels with broken wings, disguised by charms and holy words, could lead others astray.

The winter morning fog mixed with smoke from the streets as vendors set up their tables, coffee and cakes served to lines of taxi passengers. The city smelled foul, like forgotten things decaying and lost souls drifting far from home. Here, you die many deaths—and the worst is when you die while still breathing. Times were hard. These millennium years had not favoured most, except for corrupt officials or those profiting from it. My father had once told me, whether I cared for politics or not, politics always cared for me. I clenched my fists thinking of great leaders who fell to greedy men, of rules made by dishonest hands while slum dwellers suffered.

"Thinking too hard, I see," Jasmine said.

I glanced at her. She wore her favourite purple and grey tracksuit, white Nikes, and her long black hair tied neatly in a ponytail.

"Nah, not really. Just checking out the weather," I replied.

She came closer, hugging me from behind and kissing my shoulder. Her sweet scent made me forget the city's stench entirely. I turned to embrace her as she rested her head on my chest.

"Sorry I went out without telling you," She said, a hint of silliness in her voice, "I just couldn't wake you; you were sleeping so peacefully last night."

I smiled and kissed the top of her head. "It's fine Hun. I wasn't really up for jogging anyway."

She hesitated, her eyes flicking back to the street below. "I love this city, you know," she whispered, almost to herself. "But sometimes I feel like it keeps asking for pieces of us. Like the more you give, the less of you comes back but something has to be done." She looked up at me, half a smile, half a warning.

After a moment, I released her. "Speaking of sweat, before I smell like you, let me bathe and prepare for work."

She punched me lightly. "Would you like anything special for breakfast?"

I held the door, paused, and then turned with a grin. "Well— could you put yourself on a plate, all covered in that sauce I like?"

She laughed, and I winked. "Anything you prepare will do Hun."

As I prepared the bath, my thoughts drifted to her. We'd met three months ago while I jogged in the park. Her beauty struck me immediately—raven black hair tied in a neat ponytail, stretching gracefully. Her eyes, a rare blend of grey and blue, froze me in place. Her skin was smooth, like melted vanilla ice cream. Her body perfectly shaped, curves in all the right places. She was short, so I towered above her, noticing her soft, luscious lips parting as I struggled to speak. I introduced myself, and here we were.

Jasmine was smart, beautiful, and unaffected by the city's chaos. She had spent most of her life here, visiting her parents' homeland abroad only occasionally. Joburg could be hell, yet she thrived in it. We shared dreams—mine grand, hers simple—but I didn't mind. The life I wanted could coexist with what we had now.

A knock on the door pulled me from my thoughts. Jasmine stormed in, heading straight to the toilet. I jumped from my relaxed position, startled. She laughed, covering part of her face. "Don't worry, it's not number two."

We laughed.

After the usual morning antics, we returned to the bedroom.

I asked, "Is this real?"

She smiled, guiding my hand gently. "Every single beat is for you." Then, almost as if she caught herself being too vulnerable, she added with a playful roll of her eyes: "Besides, someone has to keep you from looking like a lost hobo." "I love you, Jazz," I said. "Her smile and quick kiss spoke more than words could. "You better get moving then," she said. That was enough.

Dressed, I headed to the kitchen. My bachelor pad was simple: open-plan kitchen, black and silver cupboards made by my friend Mavundla, a black L-shaped couch, glass coffee table on a red carpet, and a 50-inch plasma. The colourful paintings and pot plants were Jasmine's touch to brighten my life. She sat on the couch watching TV.

"I'm going to my place today, love. My parents are visiting, so I need to fix a few things," she said.

I nodded, but she lingered, remote in hand, eyes distant for a second. "My dad always says the city makes or breaks you. I want him to see that I'm not just surviving it—I'm shaping it." Then she caught herself, flashed her easy grin. "Anyway, don't forget to eat, Mr."

"Okay hun. I'll call when I'm settled at work. Enjoy your day." I kissed her goodbye.

Walking to the elevator, I saw Mubanga, my Nigerian neighbour and sort-of friend. Tall, dark, athletic, with a deep voice like a movie narrator. His tattoo peeked out from under his shirt, tribal and mysterious.

"Mubanga the giant," I said, raising my hand up high dramatically.

"Ah, my dwarf friend. Where are the others? Or did you leave them with Snow?" he whispered the last words, cautious Jasmine wouldn't hear.

We laughed, exchanged jokes, and I pressed the elevator button. I checked my phone as the lift descended. The screen flickered, distorted like a lost signal, and then the power cut off.

Panic surged. Alone, trapped in the dark, my head split with pain. Blood trickled from my nose. I sank to my knees, trying to steady myself, but the world twisted in red, blue, and sparks. A crackling sound filled my skull, then a popping in my ears like emerging from underwater.

Everything went black.

I felt weightless, floating in nothingness. Then a voice whispered, distant yet near.

"Finally," it said.

"Still weak," it added, echoing around me.

"Is somebody there?" I asked, trying to sound strong.

"Wake up. It's time to begin," the voice said, and an electric surge ran through me. Sparks filled the darkness. Metal clanged faintly, voices whispered, growing louder. Familiar voices, faces.

Mubanga appeared from above, guiding me with a harness.
Two paramedics pulled me out, needles stinging, oxygen mask
over my mouth. Through it all, Jasmine hovered above, tears in
her eyes. She reached out as if to touch me, her whisper
trembling: "Don't you dare leave me."

I tried to respond, but the drugs held me down.

And then, a whisper in my head:
"I sense Abelumbi—White witches."

Chapter 2

I was rushed to Millpark Private Hospital, Jasmine following the ambulance in her car. The doctors examined me, admitted me for further testing, and took blood samples. Apparently I had to be sedated since I was violently shaking. Strangely, every test showed I was in perfect health. No problems. No irregularities.

I won't lie, once the drugs wore off I felt fine—better than fine. But something was off. My appetite had changed completely. Food tasted different, richer, and sharper, like my tongue was awake for the first time. It was as if hunger had been reborn in me.

Jasmine sat by my bedside while the nurses fussed. Her jacket was folded neatly over the chair, hair slightly frizzed from rushing behind the ambulance. She tried to look calm, scrolling through her phone, but every so often her eyes darted to the machines, checking if I was still breathing normally. When I caught her staring, she smiled faintly.
"Don't scare me like that again," she whispered.
I reached for her hand. "I'll try not to."

I insisted she go home and rest, especially since her parents were visiting. She promised to pass by in the morning before heading to the airport. Her reluctance showed in the way she lingered by the door, almost turning back, before finally leaving.

Once she left, I asked the doctors about the nosebleed. Most brushed me off, telling me to wait for full results the next day. But one doctor lingered.

Doctor Langa.

He was chubby, short, dark-skinned, with a clean shave and a tiny voice that didn't fit his broad face. Mid-thirties maybe. He looked at me with concern—but there was excitement in his eyes too, as though I were a case study he couldn't wait to unpack.

"Not only was blood flowing from your nose," he said, leaning closer, "but also from your ears. Yet the MRI revealed nothing. No internal bleeding, no brain trauma." He paused, lowering his voice. "Your heart even showed signs of a minor attack— but again, no trace of damage."

He was strangely talkative, open in a way most doctors avoided. I appreciated it, but it left me unsettled. His words explained nothing.

So I tried a different approach. I told him about the voice, about how it all began in the elevator.

His face shifted, conflicted between science and belief. Then, almost reluctantly, he shared something personal. His cousin, he said, once underwent a traditional ritual overseen by African witch doctors. Strange things happened during and after. "Apparently, you become one of them at the end," he admitted, "but only if you have the calling."

He shrugged, apologizing with his eyes. "Sounds strange coming from me, I know. Off the record, though—you might want to look it up. Or speak to your family first."

Later, as he gathered his papers, I noticed the corner of a notebook sticking from his bag. He didn't realize I could see: medical diagrams half-scribbled, but on the margin—words in messy handwriting: *"What's the point of studying if I can't save more lives? I need to do more."* His lips moved faintly as he rubbed his tired eyes, muttering the same line under his breath. For a second, he was no longer the confident doctor lecturing me, but a man battling his own doubt. When he caught me looking, he straightened quickly, masking it with a thin smile.

That night, after a heavy meal the doc insisted on ordering before he left, I fell into a deep sleep. But something pulled me awake. Sweat drenched my gown. Worse—I might have pissed myself. The dream I had was so real it clung to me like smoke.

I dreamt of an African rock python coiled around me as I lay in the same hospital bed. Its massive body pressed me down, cold scales brushing the exposed parts of my gown. On its crown, a large spearhead scar glistened. Its eyes locked with mine—unblinking, unmerciful.

The snake moved slowly, seductively, studying me. I couldn't breathe. My chest froze. It opened its mouth wide, fangs flashing, jaws stretching as though it would swallow me whole.

And then—a strip of brown band fell from its mouth, drifting toward my face. Before it could touch me, I shut my eyes.

I woke with a scream, frantically wiping my body as though fleas covered me.

The room was quiet. Dimly lit. Empty except for a side table, medical equipment, and the two drips still hooked to me. Bare feet on the cold floor, I bent to check under the bed.

My heart nearly stopped.

A wristband lay there—made of snakeskin.

I didn't dare touch it. I stayed awake scanning the whole room with my eyes until morning, waiting for light, waiting for release.

Luckily, I was discharged early. The tests again showed nothing. Nothing at all. Relief washed over me, but fear lingered. If this continued, I would need help.

I phoned Jasmine before she arrived, letting her know I'd been released. She sounded relieved, though I sensed disbelief in her voice. Maybe that's why she invited me to dinner with her parents that very evening. I agreed knowing she wanted to keep an eye on me.

Then I called my boss. I needed distraction—anything to keep my mind off what was happening. They allowed me to attend a live taping of one of our shows. Not as a consultant, but as part of the audience. The program was political, watched by millions. I wasn't into politics, but it would keep me busy.

A meter taxi took me home first so I could shower and change. The cold water felt liberating, washing the hospital sweat away. On the way to the studio, we passed a body under a silver blanket, yellow police tape fluttering in the breeze. It was almost routine now in Joburg. A drunken vagrant? A mugging victim? I shivered. It could have been me. Or someone I loved.

At work, the difference was clear. Security had multiplied. Gone were the lax checks; this time I was thoroughly searched, phone switched off, ID verified. Escorted to my seat, I realized something unusual was happening.

"Is the president coming?" I asked a colleague.

He grinned like a child. "We expected his secretary, but his Excellency decided to bless us with his presence."

The atmosphere buzzed. Adjustments were made to the set at the president's request. My boss waved me to relax—"You're a guest today, just enjoy." I ended up seated with a clear view of the stage, close to the president himself.

When the show began, the presenter introduced him with booming energy. The crowd erupted; clapping like their team had just scored a goal.

There was no specific topic. Discussions meandered between party victories, history, and development. To me, it was nothing but ass-kissing. I tuned out—until I heard a voice.

"Young man," the president said, pointing at me.

Startled, I stood. "Me, sir?"

"Yes, you. Anything you'd like to add?"

The room went silent. Everyone stared. My stomach twisted.

"Please forgive me," I said carefully. "What topic are we focused on?"

Gasps. Chuckles.

He smiled. "Say whatever comes to mind, son. Anything at all concerning South Africa. Unless you'd like this opportunity to pass."

Something snapped inside me. I stepped forward, steadying my voice.

"Thank you for this honour, your excellency. My name is Mpande Mthimkhulu, proud citizen of South Africa, residing in Gauteng."

I paused. The image of the lifeless body on the street flashed in my mind. Anger surged.

"We've come far since the days of oppression. We're grateful for sacrifices made by your party and the people. But sir—your party has replaced one bad system with the same failing system. Only now it's covered in chocolate, disguised as freedom, to make it look sweet."

Murmurs rippled through the audience. My boss's jaw dropped.

The president raised his hand, silencing the room. "Please, elaborate."

And I did. I spoke of inequality, corruption, stolen billions, assets still owned by those we once fought against. I questioned what our grandparents had died for. My voice grew stronger with each word.

When I finished, the president coughed lightly. "I see you do have much to say, Mr. Mthimkhulu. Forgive me for cutting you short, but time is against us. Submit a letter of appointment to my office and I will grant you audience."

Then he turned to the crowd. "But first—let's applaud this young man. South Africa needs more like him."

The crowd erupted. The president's charisma was undeniable. He spoke with grace, sharing his story, his sacrifices, his vision of a rainbow nation. His words stirred even me, though I clung to my doubts.

Then it hit me.

A shock wave ripped through my body. I stumbled, nearly collapsing, caught by my colleague.

"You okay?" he asked.

I nodded weakly, though fear twisted my insides. It was happening again—like the elevator.

I noticed her then.

A woman in a grey suit approached the president, whispered something in his ear, then walked directly toward me. Her eyes locked onto mine, unblinking, steady. She moved through the crowd like water, her perfume wrapping around me.

She slipped an arm around me casually, guiding me as though we were friends. "The president would like a quick word," she whispered. Calm. Professional.

I could barely breathe. My energy shifted the moment I stood near the president again. He smiled warmly, teeth perfect, hand extended.

"My advisor seems to have an effect on men," he chuckled.

I shook his hand, forcing a crooked smile.

"Mr. Mthimkhulu, I'd like to personally invite you to a summit we'll be hosting with leaders from other nations. The focus will be change." His tone was serious now. "It will be in a few months. My secretary will send you details. But—tell no one. Lives depend on it."

Before I could answer, the woman in grey returned. She whispered in his ear. He nodded, and then turned to me. "I must leave now. I hope we meet again soon." He exited with his entourage.

The woman in grey stayed. She led me to an empty boardroom, closed the door, and in one swift motion shackled my hand to the table. The steel bit into my wrist.

Her voice changed—sharp, animal-like. "Who are you? Where have you been? Who are you in contact with?"

I stammered, confused.

Her eyes narrowed. "We'll have answers, at any cost. Not much reflects in our database. And I know what you are." She leaned closer, lips curling. "You're not fooling anyone." She paused at the door, unpinning the badge from her jacket. With a flick, the sharp tip kissed my skin, drawing a bead of blood. She caught it on the badge and handed it to the witch waiting in the shadows. The woman raised it to her tongue, shivering as the taste struck. The White Witch's smile was thin, satisfied.

"Do you feel it? The boy's blood is not his own," she whispered. "It belongs to a line we silenced once before. He must not walk free." Her gaze hardened, voice dropping into command. "Summon the Council. Tonight. They must taste for themselves what he carries."

She snarled, then stormed out, leaving me chained and trembling.

In the silence, a voice echoed in my head—clearer this time.

"She is a White Witch."

Chapter 3 – Part 1

"We must hurry," the voice urged. The shackles clicked open and fell from my wrists.

"Her spell is weak—she cannot hold you for long. But I cannot waste energy on her. Every drop must be saved for the road ahead," it continued, calm but firm.

I stood frozen, hands trembling as they crept to my head. My eyes darted to the shackles lying cold on the table, proof of what I had just escaped.

"There is no time to stand still!" the voice roared. "Run!"

I jolted into motion, bursting through the door—only to find three massive men in black suits advancing toward me. Their hands dipped for their guns the second I faltered. My body chose for me—I spun and sprinted, my legs hammering against the floor as I rounded the first corner.

The corridor spilled into a crowd. People shuffled toward the exit, slow, oblivious, in my way. I shoved past them, crashing into shoulders, almost falling. Every few seconds I risked a glance back. The men were there, steady and deliberate, not rushing—predators who knew their prey was already caught.

I slammed through the glass exit doors so hard the world seemed to stop and stare. My body stumbled down the stairway, flying more than running. At the bottom I spun left and right, panic flooding me. Too many eyes. Too many strangers. It felt like every one of them was watching me.

"Mpande!"

The voice was not in my head—it came from the crowd. I turned and saw the doctor, his hand raised high, snakeskin bracelet dangling. "You left this at the hospital," he called.

My stomach dropped. My heart clawed at my chest."Shit! I don't want that!" I shouted, stumbling backward before bolting the other way.

"Stop!" The voice in my head barked with sudden force. Pain ripped through my skull, dropping me to a stagger. "You need that bracelet! "I pressed my palms to my temples, teeth gritted. Desperation burned through me.

I spun back toward the doctor, my body exploding forward. My speed surprised even me—cheetah-fast, reckless. The doctor barely had time to blink before I slammed into him, ripping the bracelet from his hand.

Up the staircase above us, she appeared—the White Witch. No longer draped in grey. Her gown shimmered white, her body half-real, half-haze. People walked through her as though she were a mirage. She raised her hand, fingers pointed straight at me.

Instinct roared. I yanked the doctor's arm. "Where's your car?"

He didn't answer—just dragged me to the left, fumbling for keys with his free hand. A red sedan chirped to life.

We dove inside the car. The engine coughed, and then roared. Tires screeched. The city blurred past us as I twisted in my seat, staring through the rear-view. Nothing. No one followed.

"Relax," the voice whispered in my head, softer now. "No one is chasing you."

I flinched so hard the doctor swerved. "Damn it! Stop talking to me!" I snapped, clutching my chest.

The doctor pulled the car over. His eyes searched mine, wide with concern. "Mpande... I don't know what's happening to you, but this has to stop. You need serious help."

I struggled to catch my breath, every inhale like glass in my lungs. "I'm sorry—I don't know what's happening either."

He let out a long breath. "Should I call someone? Take you to the hospital? To a friend? Anyone?"

"No hospitals," I said quickly. "Please. I'll be fine. Just let me out."

He looked at me for a long moment, pity softening his face. "It's no trouble. Let me at least drop you somewhere safe—home, maybe."

His kindness cracked something in me. I nodded. "Thank you."

As the city swallowed us, calm seeped in. He spoke of the bracelet—how he'd been fascinated, taken a picture, sent it to his cousin. How his cousin had called him back immediately, panicked, begging him to return it. Fate had led him here—he'd recognized me on a hospital broadcast, rushing to deliver it. He even scribbled his cousin's number for me. "If anyone can help, it's him," he said.

I had him drop me off at Bree Street, far from home. Extra precaution. Less chance he'd be questioned.

"Truly," I told him as I climbed out, "I'm grateful."

I waited for him to leave, ducked into the first building, then called a meter taxi.

When the cab was only two streets away from Esselene, the voice returned, gentler this time, as if tapping the inside of my mind.

"I hope you are not going to the apartment."

"Why?" I muttered aloud.

The driver glanced back. "What?"

"Sorry—I talk to myself sometimes."

"You don't need to speak," the voice said with a smirk that wasn't a smirk. "Just think it. I'm in your mind."

I clenched my jaw. "Great. A comedian in my head."

"You know more than you think," it replied, almost laughing. "But for now—do not go home."

The taxi stopped. The driver asked, "Is this the place?"

The voice's tone hardened. "Do you value your life?"

I handed the driver his fee and changed the destination. My head throbbed. My heart begged for quiet.

"I was invited to dinner," I thought. "I need peace. Just one meal. Then we can talk."

Silence.

When the car rolled to a stop again, I climbed out before doubt could drag me back. The townhouse near Killarney Mall stood proud, its stone walls aged but timeless, garden blooming in perfect order. The pathway crunched beneath my shoes as I rang the bell.

Footsteps.

The door swung open and Jasmine's smile lit everything. She wrapped me in her arms, kissed me softly.

"You're early," she teased. "But we're ready. Come in."

The warm smell of food floated down the hallway. My stomach growled, reminding me how empty it was. I followed her past the kitchen, into the lounge.

"Mum, Dad," she called.

Two figures turned toward us.

"Oh. My. God." Jasmine's mother clutched her chest, eyes wide with horror.

The voice in my head stiffened. "What the—"

Jasmine's father shot up from his seat, pulling his wife close.Her mother's voice cracked with panic. "How could you bring this thing here? Do you know what he is? Oh God, Jasmine!".

Chapter 3 – Part 2

Jasmine's father's voice thundered—not with sound, but inside my skull.

You! What do you want here? Have you come to kill us?

My breath caught. "What is going on? And no!" I shouted out loud, my voice breaking the air.

Jasmine stared at me, shock rippling through her face. She didn't speak, but her eyes screamed the question: *What are you hiding from me?*

"Get this thing out of here!" her mother cried, her voice sharp with hatred.

"He is not a thing!" Jasmine's voice cracked. She moved closer to me, slipping half a step in front of my shoulder as though she could shield me. "Mum, Dad, what the hell is going on?! He's kind, he's human—he's mine!"

"Calm down," her father said, steady but commanding. His hand tightened on his wife's. "Jane—trusts me."

The silence that followed was thick enough to choke on.

Abelumbi, the voice in my head whispered. It had never sounded so guarded.

Jasmine's father locked his eyes on me. *Why do you look so frightened? Why do you play at confusion, when a protector of such power coils within you?*

I had no answer. None.

"Jasmine," her father said gently, turning toward her, "sit down.
I promise we'll explain everything. But first—I need a word
with your friend."

Jasmine lowered herself onto the couch, her hands trembling.
Even then, her gaze never left me. It was a gaze that said: *I
don't care what they think you are. I see you.*

He motioned for me to sit as well. Reluctantly, I did.

"I'll be plain with you," he said. "Do you know us?"
I shook my head.
"Do you know what we are?"
I nodded.

His wife's eyes cut through me, unreadable, but heavy with
meaning.

"Does Jasmine know what you are?" he asked softly. "Does she
know what you carry with you?"

I stared at their faces, desperate for answers that weren't there.
My chest burned. Finally, I exhaled and let the truth spill out.

"I don't know what's happening. It started last night with a
voice in my head, and since then—chaos. I was chased today
by one of your kind. Yes a White Witch.. That's how I know
what you are. But I'm done. I'm exhausted. Hungry. All I
wanted was to meet the parents of my girlfriend, then rest.
That's it."

I turned to Jasmine, my voice breaking softer. "Babe, I love
you. I never imagined meeting your parents would go like this.
But… goodbye."

I rose to leave.

"You saw a White Witch?" Jasmine gasped behind me her voice sharp with recognition. As though something old inside her had stirred awake. "Did you just say White Witch?"

Her mother stood and snapped her fingers twice. Jasmine collapsed unconscious onto the couch.

Rage flared in me. "What did you do to her?!"

Her mother's hands danced in the air, lips chanting words I couldn't understand. Power surged like a crushing tide, pressing down on me—smothering me. My ribs felt like they would snap.

Instinct saved me. My hand flew to the bracelet. A python erupted, coiling around me, shielding me. The weight vanished. Light blazed from my eyes.

The voice in my head spoke through my mouth, booming with unnatural force:

"Try me."

Jasmine's father stepped forward, lifting his hand. "Jane! Stop. Let him leave."

Her mother froze, fury burning in her eyes.

Her father's gaze turned to me. "Please. Leave. And as a father—I beg you—stay away from my daughter. We've hidden the truth for years, hoping she could live normally. If you love her… let her go."

The voice inside me growled back. "She has come of age, Johnson. She must accept her birth right."

He shook his head. "We know. But not like this. We will erase her memory, and reveal the truth carefully. That is our duty."

The voice fell quiet, beaten. *Very well,* it said.

Suddenly I was outside, the python shrinking back into the bracelet around my wrist. My knees buckled. Behind me, the door opened. Jasmine's father appeared, watching me with eyes heavy with pity.

A rush of air—and he was beside me, lifting me by the arm.

"Relax," he said gently. "I won't harm you."

The bracelet itched, alive under my skin.

"You boys don't know how to care for yourselves anymore," he muttered. "Come. Eat something. Then you can go."

Too weak to protest, I let him guide me back inside.

The table was set with a feast fit for royalty. Jasmine did not join us. Her absence stung like a fresh wound, but I swallowed the pain. I ate quietly, avoiding her mother's eyes.

After a long silence, her father spoke. "What is your name, young man?"

"Mpande," I said.

"Mpande," he repeated, as though tasting the weight of it. "You must understand—we'll have to report this to the Witch's Council."

My fork stilled. "Is that... bad?"

He chuckled softly, pouring himself whisky. "Forgive me. It's just—people spend years meditating, training, bleeding, and still they can't reach a fraction of the energy you command. And yet here you sit, unaware of what you are."

He pushed a glass to me. I drank. It burned fire down my chest.

"But yes," he continued. "Reporting you is dangerous for you. Not reporting is dangerous for us—especially Jasmine. The Council will find you. It is only a matter of time."

He leaned closer. "Tell me, Mpande—what history do you learn here, in South Africa? What do you know of your heritage?"

I opened my mouth to answer, but his wife slammed her hand on the table, rattling the plates.

"Enough!" she snapped. "He leaves. Now."

Her eyes were knives.

I pushed my chair back, drained the last of the whisky, and stood. My chest ached, but my voice was steady.

"Thank you," I said, and walked out into the night.

Sadness pressed down on me, but somewhere inside, I knew— one day, all of this would make sense.

Chapter 4

I walked for a while before calling a taxi. The voice was silent for the rest of the night. Instead of going back to my apartment, I booked a room near the Braamfontein bus station. Sleep came easily, and nothing out of the ordinary disturbed me.

In the morning, I reached for my phone, ready to call Indaba Org, when the voice finally spoke.
"Do not tell anyone of your whereabouts. And I believe Lisa Mthimkhulu should be your first priority," it said, faint and weak.

"What's with you today? And how do you know my mum?" I asked. I had grown used to having a voice in my head—strange as that sounded. Only two days had passed, yet it felt almost natural.

"I know everything about you. And just so you know, I must save energy. I used too much during that display at the Johnsons' house," the voice replied.

"Oh, about that—thank you. If it wasn't for you, I don't know what would have become of me," I said.

"No need," it answered, weaker still.

"Do you want to rest? And come to think of it, I don't even know your name."

"The Voice is fine. That's what you call me, isn't it?" It almost sounded like laughter, faint and distant. "To save energy, I'll send information and direction through dreams. Hope you're good at interpreting them."

I laughed alone, unsure how to respond.

After preparing for the journey ahead, the voice fell silent again. My mother lived miles from the city, and it had been months since I'd last seen her. Lisa Mthimkhulu was my adoptive parent. Her late husband, Albert Nguni—the only man I had ever known as a father. She then remarried, Arthur Mbazo, and together they had sold our old home to buy a farm in the Vaal.

Relief washed over me as I left the city behind. My body felt lighter, as if a burden had slipped from my shoulders. The further south we travelled, the more I wished never to return to that cursed city. I dozed off in the taxi and drifted into my first dream.

It wasn't as clear as I expected, but at least it wasn't a nightmare. An old man appeared—bald, with a long white beard, clad in Zulu attire, holding a spear and shield. He stood on a riverbank, and I watched from behind the bushes. Then he turned and walked into the river. I panicked, fearing he would drown, and rushed forward.

But a lion blocked my way, jaws dripping fresh blood. The beast crouched, ready to leap. Just then, a star plummeted from the heavens, blazing faster than any craft. Small, no bigger than a soccer ball, it landed in the river. Before it touched the water, the old man leapt and caught it with ease. Emerging from the river, he stood beside the lion.

Drums echoed all around. My heartbeat matched their rhythm. The old man bowed and extended the glowing star toward me. I stepped forward, reaching out to accept it, when the light grew so bright my eyes burned.

I blinked—and woke in the taxi. A woman beside me crunched on snacks. We were nearing my stop.

I had a long walk ahead, as no taxis ran toward the scattered farms. Luckily, I carried no luggage, and the fresh Vaal air felt like a blessing. No traffic, no foul stench, no choking smoke— just quiet. For once, I could hear my thoughts clearly.

At last, I reached the farmhouse. The Mbazo's welcomed me warmly. My mum, Mr. Mbazo, and his two sons were overjoyed. To my surprise, almost a year had passed since I last saw my mum. Even more shocking—she had given birth to a baby girl, only weeks old.

Joy overwhelmed me as I held the tiny bundle in my arms. She was perfect. Mbalenhle, they called her—a beautiful flower. I now had a little sister, as well as two younger brothers.

My days there reminded me of what family meant. Time in the countryside seemed to move slower, yet I wished it would slow even more. A week passed quickly, and soon my stay was cut short by another dream.

This time, I sought guidance from Mthobisi, Dr. Langa's cousin, whom I had stayed in contact with. His advice was sharp, though his request puzzled me—he wanted to join my journey, to witness how it unfolded. If I succeeded, he wished to be my student. I agreed. He would travel by bus from Durban, arriving at noon the next day. He was also bringing a friend, a guide who knew the river we sought.

When I explained everything to my mum, including the voice in my head, she listened with concern but gave me her full support. She feared for my safety, but still took the beaded wristband for protection. I didn't have the heart to tell her it was tied to a giant snake. Thankfully, I doubted anyone searching for me could connect her to me, given how broken the records were after her remarriage.

That night, we gathered around the dinner table. Laughter filled the room, mostly at my expense. They teased me about my clumsy attempts at farm life—falling off a horse, nearly being kicked by a cow, almost tumbling out of a boat at the Vaal Dam. Despite the embarrassment, I felt happy. Truly happy.

Later, as I helped my mum clean up, her sadness showed. She asked me to stay, to abandon this path. I had thought of it many times, but deep down, I knew I couldn't. The voice had awakened, and with it came a truth I couldn't ignore: if I turned away, sickness and death would eventually claim me before anyone figured out what was wrong. That much had been made painfully clear.

That night I learned of the portal. Every twenty years, it opened in different parts of Africa. Only a chosen few could pass through. One of my ancestors had done so centuries ago, leaving behind traces in my bloodline. Though our clan was not well known, my first gift had already made me stronger than most. The tragedy was that others had prepared their whole lives for such journeys, while I was still untested.

Dreams showed me glimpses of the portal's path, and sometimes the trials awaiting me. To claim more gifts, I would have to face challenges—deadly ones. Enemies had long tried to erase us from history, hunting down bloodlines like mine. Some even betrayed their own people for survival.

As I pondered this, sleep finally claimed me.

The next morning, I rose early, nerves tight in my chest. "I am ready," I whispered, drawing a deep breath. After saying my goodbyes, I met Mthobisi at the N1 garage as planned.

Among the crowd, he and his companion stood out in their traditional attire. Beaded necklaces in red and white hung around Mthobisi's neck, some threaded with animal skin. His long dreadlocks were tipped with beads, and his black-and-white outfit gave him a commanding presence. His companion wore cowhide, a leopard-print vest, and carried twin sticks.

We greeted each other warmly, as though we had known each other for years. Mthobisi introduced his friend: Lunga Zwane, a short man about my height, with tattoos I couldn't make out and a grip like steel.

From there, the plan unfolded. We hitchhiked as far as Bloemfontein, and then continued on foot, Lunga leading the way. Along the Orange River, Mthobisi collected herbs guided by his ancestors. I wondered if they spoke to him the way the Voice spoke to me.

The journey was gruelling. Nights were cold, the jungle thick, and fear gnawed at me—I had never camped before. Yet my companions treated me like family, and it eased the weight of it all.

By the time we reached the riverbank, the Voice urged me forward. Hunger clawed at me, and exhaustion dragged at my steps. That was when we saw him.

A man stood ahead, wearing nothing but a white cloth around his waist. Tall, scarred, and muscular, he looked like a warrior forged in countless battles. His eyes locked on us, unblinking.

"I am the gate guard, Nkhanyamba," he thundered, "and only the one who bears the glow of Nkhanyezi may pass."

Lunga stepped forward, but the guard raised his hand. "Not you, child. I appear only because of him," he said, pointing at me.

Fear clawed at me, but I stepped forward. My companions could go no further. The guard explained they must return to civilization and drink from the river before leaving, lest they be lost forever. Grateful yet saddened, I bid them farewell.

I followed Nkhanyamba in silence, his presence heavy, the air thick with unseen power. Leopards appeared along the way—seven of them, their eyes glowing.

"These are kings of old," the guard said. "Their spirits inhabit these creatures, to protect us after the Witch Hunt scattered our people."

We passed unnoticed by ordinary travellers, for the guard explained that ancient spirits walked with us, hidden from human sight. My heart beat faster as the air grew warmer, charged with unseen energy.

Finally, he stopped. "Behold. The portal of Nkhanyezi."

I saw only river and trees. Yet I felt it—something vast and alive, pressing against my soul.

"Rest," the guard said. "Your journey begins at midnight."

That night, we made a fire. He sang in a deep, sorrowful voice. The leopards drew near, and the Voice in my head joined the song. A tear slipped down my cheek. Then the river shimmered with colour, a rainbow forming over the water as a star glowed above us.

"You are remarkable, Mpande," the guard said. "You see what others die before beholding. Nkhanyezi has shed a tear for you. Do not waste it."

When midnight came, he ordered me to strip off my clothes. The cold stung my skin, but I obeyed.

I stepped into the river and swam to the centre. Above me, the star's tear fell. It struck with a force beyond imagination, dragging me under. Water rushed into my mouth and nose, my lungs burning, my body convulsing.

"Relax," the Voice whispered. "Submit. Do not fight it."

So I let go. And I sank deeper into the dark.

Chapter 5 — Part 1

When I opened my eyes, I was still in the river, but now it was daylight. The water felt warm, and the trees were thicker, greener, surrounding me like a hidden world. I swam to the riverbank and took a deep breath. The air smelled different from the last time I inhaled it.

I scanned the area for the guard—and a leopard appeared. I smiled, waved at it, and looked around for the others, but saw none. It approached slowly, stalking me, pausing with deliberate intent.

"Run!" The voice in my head screamed.

I bolted, my legs moving faster than ever. I could feel the power of its paws pounding behind me. A roar split the air. I didn't dare look back, climbing the nearest tree, gripping the top branch with everything I had. My heart pounded like a drum.

Movement below caught my eye. A figure appeared, then another.

"Hey! You there!" a voice called. "Climb down."

Fear froze me. My heart still racing, I stayed put.

"Little boy, climb down—the leopard is dead. It won't harm you," said the man.

It took a gentle hand and encouragement to convince me to descend. When I hit the ground, my knees buckled. I looked at the beast laying there with a spear protruding from it. I fell and fainted.

A splash of water woke me. Around me stood a group of men—some amused, some serious. I coughed, bewildered, trying to understand who they were.

"Tell me, boy," one said sharply, "why would you wave at a leopard and stand?"

I froze. Then laughter erupted from the group, and I joined in, uneasy but relieved.

"We'll head back to the village when the other scouts arrive for the night shift," the man continued. "You're very lucky, son. My name is Bongani Ntuli. I'm the leader of the hyena group."

I shook his hand cautiously. "My name is Mpande, and… thank you for saving my life, sir."

Bongani introduced me to his fifteen men. We set up camp near the mountains. Around the fire, they shared food—springbok, rabbits, and stories of battles from the Lion group. Tales of bravery and danger, some hard to believe. Everyone seemed eager to join the Lion group, drawn by fame, respect, and perks.

It was only then I noticed my own nakedness. A man handed me a cowhide apron to cover myself.

The hyena group treated me well, though the leopard's death had earned them prestige—its organs taken, skin prepared for ceremonial use. Replacement scouts arrived late, disrespect in their posture.

We made our way back to the village. Darkness enveloped everything. My eyes struggled to adjust, while the men navigated effortlessly.

"Why is it so dark?" I asked in my mind.

The voice laughed. "You inhabit the body of a fourteen-year-old who lived hundreds of years before you were born. Your modern lights do not exist here."

I chuckled.

"And why is everyone speaking English?" I asked next.

"Your mind translates it all for clarity," the voice explained. "You don't know Nguni in its purest form. The language of your time has lost much of our heritage."

"So this is all in my mind?" I asked.

"Partly. You feel everything, must eat, live, experience—but much is reanimated within your consciousness."

"Whose body am I in?"

"You are reliving the life of your great-great-great-grandfather—Mpande Nkosi—who lived over five centuries ago. His spirit chose to share the light of Khanyezi with you."

I struggled to grasp it all, though the voice made it seem simple.

"This path will prepare you mentally, physically, and spiritually," it said. "Someone else entering this portal would face their own trials, in their own vessel."

Back in the village, a voice cut through the dark: "Mpande!"

Startled, I froze. "That's your father," the voice said. "Nkosi, a former king's guard and respected man here."

He arrived, wasting no time, striking me across the back of my head. Stars danced before my eyes. Bongani stepped in between us. His men bowed.

"Step back, child. Don't be fooled by this cane," my father said, voice commanding. "I can take all of you down without breaking a sweat."

Fear clamped my chest. I could barely stand.

"Forgive me, sir," Bongani said, and the men stepped aside further.

My father's grip lifted me, one hand on my shoulder, the other holding his cane for balance. "Where did you find him?"

"At the river near the mountains, sir," a man replied.

A beating followed. I screamed and kicked, but he said nothing, dragging me to a large hut, lit by a single fire.

"Where are the sheep and cattle, Mpande?" he demanded.

I sat, numb from pain. "I do not know."

Silence fell. Then he exhaled sharply, taking a seat across the room. "Wash yourself near the fire," he said, pointing to a clay bowl.

I obeyed, my body aching, the smoke curling around me. He served porridge and meat. We ate in silence. The voice, unusually, remained quiet.

That night, I slept on a thin mat by the fire. I dreamed of cornfields and a calling voice, only to wake with a clay bucket hurled at me. My father's presence loomed, pipe in mouth, anger simmering, reminding me of my duties.

Morning came with the usual barrage—fetches water, feed chickens, milk cows, clear the yard, lead the herd. The voice chuckled softly, noting my little rebellion over the lost livestock. I rushed out, bread in hand, careful to accept it correctly—or so the voice explained.

Customs, chores, and survival were now my reality.

Chapter 5 — Part 2

Days blurred into weeks. My father's constant scrutiny never eased. Every task I did seemed insufficient, no matter how hard I tried. He smoked his pipe, muttering criticisms under his breath, as if my existence itself was a failure.

The village kids paid me little attention, none showing interest in friendship. I barely noticed, my chores keeping me occupied. The air was clear, the dangerous paths avoided, but the wilderness reminded me that predators lurked beyond the familiar. A wild cat crossed my path once—a fleeting reminder that life here was fragile.

One morning, as I led the herd to greener pastures, I saw a group of older boys tormenting a smaller child. He was skinny, lighter-skinned, struggling as they forced dirt into his mouth. My herd mingled with theirs, and I realized the boy they were picking on was left behind, tears streaking his face.

The gang noticed me.

"What do we have here? Challenging me, boy?" the eldest demanded.

One of the younger boys whispered, "He's the witch's son."

Anger flared. How dare they insult my mother? I stepped forward, fists clenched, eyes locked on the group.

"Well, seems you hit the right spot, mouse. Give him sticks," the eldest commanded.

A boy hesitated but handed me sticks. I didn't know how to hold them properly. The first blow came fast, aimed at my head. I blocked, but the others followed relentlessly.

The final strike sent me crashing to the ground. Blood trickled down my forehead. Dizziness overtook me. Panic surged.

I scrambled up, tears mingling with the blood on my face, and ran. I didn't stop until I reached home, heart hammering, lungs burning.

My father sat outside; pipe in hand, expression blank.

"What's wrong, boy?" he asked.

Through sobs, I recounted the attack. His anger ignited.

"Go back there!" he barked.

My heart sank. His words cut deeper than the blows I had taken. But I obeyed, dragging myself back to the scene. The gang had vanished, their livestock gone, except mine. Confusion gnawed at me.

I rested by a pond, head on grass, asking the voice in my mind:

"What is this for? I don't understand the lessons. How is herding teaching me anything?"

"Just have faith," the voice replied.

Even with that, a gnawing emptiness settled inside me. I slept by the pond, rising only when I had to gather the herd.

Back home, the routine continued. My father's anger was relentless, his expectations unyielding. When he discovered a missing cow, his eyes darkened.

"Where is my cow, Mpande?!"

"I do not know," I said, bitterness dripping from my words.

A smack across my face followed. I stumbled, but instead of fear, defiance surged.

"Since you care so much about your animals, why don't you just stay with them? Clearly, they mean more to you than I do," I shouted, running past him.

His voice chased me, but I didn't look back. I ran toward the mountain and river, my chest heaving, my legs burning, with one thought driving me forward: to escape this life that felt meaningless. The voice in my head urged me to stop, to reconsider, but anger and despair drowned it out.

The sky darkened as I neared the river, clouds swirling like an omen above me. My feet stumbled over rocks and roots, my hands clawing at branches as if the forest itself would swallow me whole. And yet, beneath the rage and fear, something pulled me onward—a gentle, almost invisible force that whispered in a language older than my anger.

I stopped for a moment on a small rise overlooking the river below. Lightning cracked across the sky, and the roar of the rushing water filled my ears. My breathing slowed as I felt the wind against my face. And then, in the midst of the chaos, warmth settled over me, as if unseen hands were holding me back from my own destruction.

A voice—soft, familiar, impossibly warm—echoed in my mind: *"Before you die, Mpande... you must live."*

I froze. For the first time since waking in this place, I felt something more than fear or anger. Something deeper, older, and unshakably real. The river, the wind, the storm, even the shadows around me—they were calling me. Not to end, but to begin.

With trembling legs, I turned from the cliff, feeling the ancestral pull urging me forward; guiding me down the slope toward the river, toward whatever awaited me next.

Chapter 6

The wind slowed my pace, but I pushed through. Dust stung my eyes, rain began to fall, and twigs slapped my body, yet I pressed on. The jungle thickened, trees closing overhead, the path hidden. Anger boiled, but that guiding force stayed with me.

Emerging into a clearing, the river thundered below the cliff."Do not do this, Mpande," the voice said. "If you die here, there is no waking in your time, and I do not know what lies beyond."

I ignored it, letting the rain soak me, letting the storm roar through me. Lightning struck a tree, illuminating the river's wild beauty. Chaos and awe collided, and I breathed it in.

"Before you die, Mpande, you must live," a woman's voice repeated—warm, familiar, like a memory etched in my bones. The rain, the river, the scent of wet earth—it grounded me.

A hand rested lightly on my shoulder. I looked up—my father, eyes glistening with tears, standing in the storm.

"Did you hear that?" I asked. He only stared at the lightning-struck tree.
"I believe that was your mother, son. Some say her voice still chants when it rains," he said softly.

We stood there, rain pouring over us, until I whispered, "How did you find me?"
"I never lost you. You are strong and fast. It took effort to keep up," he chuckled. Then, quieter, "I am sorry for being too hard on you, son."

I realized this was the very spot my mother had died. "Let us go home, Dad," I said, taking his hand.

The rain eased on our walk back. At home, he prepared a fire and a bath. Nhlanhla arrived with food and a bucket of homemade beer, her presence comforting. Dinner passed with quiet laughter, stories of my mother, and revelations of her gifts as a healer and prophet, the sacrifices she made, and the portal she had leapt through to change history.

Mornings passed with stick training. One for defence, one for attack. He corrected my stance, taught balance, and showed how chores had already built my strength. Months passed, my skill sharpened, my mind grew sharper, and our bond deepened.

"Strength alone is not enough," he said. "The first battle begins in the mind. Believe you cannot win, and it is true. Use your brain, your body, and your spirit together. Never tell yourself you cannot."

One day, during a duel near the kraal, I struck hard. His eyes glowed white. A shadow burst from him, hitting me with a force that sent me flying. My sticks scattered; I landed hard.

"What the…what was that?" I gasped.

He laughed, smoke curling around him. "It's been a while. Let's prepare a feast." His cane was gone, his limp vanished, and energy radiated from him in a way I had never seen.

The day passed in celebration and preparation for the great harvest. That night, as the fire crackled, he spoke again:

"The spirit moves the body, animates action, and even reaches beyond. What I did today—pushed you away with my spirit—

is a power unseen but trainable. We are all part of God. Life, used wisely, opens doors you cannot yet imagine. We rest now, until the harvest passes. Then, training continues."

I slept that night, storm quieted in my mind, ready to face the lessons and trials that waited at dawn.

Jasmines Awakening

Jasmine woke up in her house, her head heavy and aching — like someone who'd drunk too much the night before.

"What's going on? And why would I sleep in my clothes?" she groaned, rubbing her temples.

Her mother, smiling softly, guided her to the couch and handed her a warm cup of tea.
"Morning, darling. You were so thrilled last night — coming back home with us — that you went a little overboard with the wine," she said, her tone sweet but distant.

Jasmine blinked, confusion deepening. Her father sat quietly in the corner, a glass of whiskey in hand.

"Me? Drinking wine? And why is Dad drinking *this* early? What time is it?" she asked.

Her mother explained how they'd had a wonderful evening — how Jasmine had laughed, cried, and spoken about the place she'd been living in. They'd all agreed she'd move back home and marry Jamie, who had already approached her parents with an offer.

"But... what about the children at the recreation center?" she asked, her voice trembling.

The words bounced around her head like echoes from a dream. None of it felt real. A dull ache bloomed in her chest — love mixed with doubt. Jamie. It was strange; she'd once believed they were meant to be, but that was a child's fantasy.

She spent the day half-listening to her mother's chatter, her body heavy with fatigue and unease. That night, when she finally drifted to sleep, she dreamed of a man she had never met — nothing like Jamie, not even close — yet she felt an inexplicable connection to him.

By morning, she was packed and sitting in the back of a taxi with her parents, bound for the airport. Her mother spoke endlessly, her father silent. Jasmine stared out the window, watching the city roll past, disappointment rising like a tide.

When they arrived, she turned to them, calm but resolute.

"Mum. Dad. I'm not coming with you — and there's nothing you can say to change my mind. I'm not angry, just... disappointed. I need time to figure things out."

Her mother tried to speak, but Jasmine lifted her hand.
"I won't listen to any more lies. And don't you *dare* try to use magic on me again, Mum."

The air went still.

"Go home," she said softly. "Know that I will find Mpande — regardless of the Witch's Council, or your part in all of it."

Without another word, she stepped into the taxi and drove away, leaving them standing in silence — uncertain, powerless, and afraid.

For the first time in what felt like ages, I dreamed of Jasmine. When I opened my eyes, the world around me hummed — neither fully mine nor entirely strange. I whispered to myself, *I am here now*, though even the air seemed to question it. This place breathes like the one I left behind, yet something unseen watches between the shadows.

I surrendered to the night's soft murmurs, letting them pull me under once more — where dreams and memory blur into one endless current.

Chapter 7

My uncle arrived early in the morning, his voice booming across the hills as he called our clan names. Father welcomed him warmly, guiding him inside, and I was introduced soon after finishing my chores. He hugged me with a grin.

"My sister's child has grown into a fine young man. Handsome too. I bet you're already popular with the ladies, like your uncle," he teased, winking.

I laughed nervously, while Father rolled his eyes. My uncle stood almost as tall as him, his lighter skin and jet-black beard giving him a younger look. He wore a black-and-white robe with a silver necklace, bronze armbands and anklets, and carried only a small animal-skin sack for provisions. Everything about him radiated confidence.

We spoke for hours as he shared tales of his travels. There was unrest brewing—one clan threatened to rebel against the Zulu king of kings. With thirteen clans under his authority, the thought of rebellion carried a dangerous weight. My uncle's Swati clan was not under the king's direct rule, but their ties to the Zulu people were strong.

By midday we joined the others in the fields. The sun burned overhead, but the air was alive with song. Villagers laughed, embraced, and worked in harmony. Even the children joined in. I hadn't realized so many people lived here, spread out as the homesteads were. It felt good to belong.

Then I saw her.

A girl so beautiful my heart skipped a beat. She moved gracefully through the workers, her smile lighting everything around her. My hands fumbled with the digging tool, and Father cleared his throat while my uncle chuckled knowingly.

He called her over, asked her name, and learned of her parents. She answered with a soft voice that made me sweat more than the sun ever could. As she passed, she looked at me and smiled.

"Boy," my uncle whispered, grinning, "I just got you her name and where she lives. The rest is up to you."

Father jabbed him in the shoulder. "Let the child be."

Later, as the fields emptied, I gathered tools and nearly collided with her again.

"Hi. My name is Gugu," she said sweetly. "Your uncle told me to tell you they'll be home late. Nhlanhla will take care of you."

She turned to go, but without thinking I reached for her hand. "Gugu… may I see you again tomorrow?"

Her eyes widened. "I don't even know you."

"My name is Mpande," I stammered. "My father is Mr. Nkosi. I live in one of the huts on the edge of the village."

She smiled, though shyly. "I live on the other side, near the river. I can't be seen with you here—my mother would beat me."

"Then where do you fetch water?" I asked quickly.

"By the bend where the river turns north. Why?"

"Meet me there?"

She hesitated, and then smiled at the ground. "I must go. But… meet me tomorrow before sunrise." She ran off, calling back, "Don't be late!"

Warmth spread through me, carrying me all the way home.

I woke before dawn. The hut was dark, but Father and my uncle were already awake, kneeling before a fire that hadn't been there moments before. Shadows flickered across their faces.

"Who lit the fire?" I asked softly.

"Don't be alarmed," Father began, but my uncle cut in with a wink. "Go about your business, Mpande. Your father would turn this into a long story, and you'd miss your girl."

I slipped out with my clay pot, smiling despite myself. The walk to the river was long, but anticipation carried me. When I reached the northern bend, she was already there, leaning against a rock.

For a moment I just stared, disbelieving she was real.

We talked for what felt like hours, laughing, trading stories, and sharing likes and dislikes as though we had known each other forever. When villagers began to arrive with buckets, she whispered that she had to go. We walked together, hands brushing, buckets swinging like rugby balls at our sides. At the riverbank she placed hers on her head and smiled.

"Until the harvest," she promised, walking away.

I watched her go, heart pounding with new energy.

But on my way back, a familiar voice stopped me. A group of boys stepped from the bush.

"Far from home, aren't you?" sneered the one who had scarred me before.

They threw me two sticks. My grip tightened.

"This isn't a duel," he mocked. "My friend saw you with his sister. None of us liked it. We'll leave you broken here in the bush. Attack!"

They rushed.

Rage ignited within me. The world slowed. I blocked the first blow and countered, striking one boy down like a sack of mealie. They had no rhythm, no unity. I parried and struck, my arms moving faster than thought. One by one, they fell.

The scarred boy's stick snapped under my strike. Fear flashed in his eyes, but I did not hesitate. My next blow landed with a sickening crack. He collapsed, screaming. Two of the boys fled into the bush. The rest lay groaning on the ground.

My chest burned, my breath ragged, but the rage still surged. I dropped the sticks, lifted my clay pot, and walked home without a word.

At the hut, I set the pot down. My hands shook. Memories of bone cracking filled my ears. I staggered to the river, dunked myself under the cold water, and emerged calmer, though not cleansed.

The next day the village pulsed with excitement. Families carried gifts, food, fabric, and drums toward the king's yard. The air was thick with the smell of roasted meat and earth. We laid our things on a mat in the open field before the king's gate, and then returned for the rest.

Suddenly, a horn sounded. Everyone stilled.

Drums began, slow at first, then building. A man emerged, singing praises of the king's lineage, his voice carrying across the field. Women trilled in joy, sweeping the ground with brooms of dried grass. The names he recited stretched back generations, and I felt the weight of history pressing on us.

Then silence.

From the gate stepped a man unlike any I had ever seen. His body was massive, his muscles carved like stone, covered only by the skins of lions. He towered above the crowd, his presence bending the air itself.

Father pulled me down beside him.

"Is that the king?" I whispered, swallowing hard.

Chapter 8

The giant man scanned the field, towering above us all. For a moment, I thought he was the king, and suddenly it made sense why the royal hut was so large, surrounded by a dozen smaller ones and a sprawling kraal with sections for every kind of livestock. A man like this could devour a sheep alone, I thought, and leave nothing but bones.

"That's not the king's son," my father said, cutting into my wandering thoughts.

I turned in surprise, looking from him to my uncle.

"That's the king's guard," my father explained with a smile.

"Bayede!" cried the praise-singer, and the whole crowd bowed.

"Greetings," a voice rang out. I dared to peek, but my father pressed me back down.

"You may rise," the king said, and the village erupted in joy.

I tried shifting left and right, squeezing between people for a glimpse, but the crowd blocked me. At last my father chuckled, placed his hand on my shoulder, and said, "Perhaps you're a little old for this, but since you're so eager..." Then, to my amazement, he lifted me onto his shoulders.

From up high, I finally saw him. Standing beside the giant guard, waving to his people, the king shone in full leopard skin from head to toe. He was handsome, commanding, and his presence carried like thunder rolling through the valley. My chest swelled. This was greatness.

He gave a short speech, then took his seat. Before him, three women knelt on the ground in perfect posture. His guard remained at his left side, eyes scanning the crowd, ever-watchful. To the right sat a row of old men, laughing and trading quiet words. The king's eldest son sat to his left, another guard standing behind him.

The youngest woman rose, fetched a bowl of water, and knelt before the king. After he washed his hands, a servant brought a great wooden plate of meat. He tore off the first piece, and the platter was passed along his family until, to my surprise, it reached the people. Servants kept refilling it, and soon the king lifted a gourd of traditional beer. Before drinking, he raised it skyward and poured a libation to the earth.

My father lowered me as the plate neared. I cannot explain the joy that filled my chest as I shared in the same food as the king. Around us, elders drank, children played, and voices rose in laughter.

My uncle tapped my shoulder, pointing with a grin I didn't understand—until I saw her. Gugu. She stood only a few steps away, her beauty beyond words. She smiled shyly, looking down, and my heart leapt.

I started forward, but my father caught my hand. "Don't vanish too long, Mpande."

"Let the child go, Nkosi. You'll embarrass him in front of the girl," my uncle teased. My father released me, and even Nhlanhla nodded with a smile.

I grinned back at them, and then hurried to Gugu. She wore a beaded dress with matching bands on her head and arms. I longed to hold her, but we were surrounded by eyes.

"Hey," I said softly.

She smiled, though her voice was heavy. "Not well. But we'll talk after my cousin's performance—she's been chosen to open the challenges."

Before I could respond, she grabbed my hand and pulled me through the crowd. We stopped near the king's family just as he rose, silencing the field with a single gesture. The praise-singer's voice soared: "Mbalenhle, the king's flower!"

A little girl stepped forward. I didn't understand the title until she began to sing. Her voice was pure, angelic. She sang of her mother, and the whole crowd was moved to tears. Soon they joined her, voices rising in unison. Even I wept. Gugu gripped my hand, and when the song ended, she tugged me away once more.

This time we slipped from the field, through thinning crowds, toward the trees behind the royal huts. We laughed as we ran into the bushes, hearts pounding. When we stopped, hidden among the trees, her face turned serious.

"My mother hates you. And my father swore he'd break your neck if he ever found you near me," she whispered.

I stiffened.

"But," she added quickly, "he only said it to please her. He wouldn't risk a fight with the great general. Besides—you broke my brother's hand."

"I… they started it. I was only carrying water when they threw sticks at me," I muttered.

She laughed. "Don't worry. They deserved it. Though Senzo got the worst of it."

"Who's Senzo?"

She giggled. "The biggest fool of them all. But he won't trouble me again, not now that we're together."

The word *together* made my heart race. I smiled as we walked hand in hand.

Soon we stumbled into a hidden paradise—a vast garden of green grass, blooming flowers, and towering trees. A stream ran through it, stones placed like a crafted park. The air smelled of blossoms, alive with birdcalls and the splash of water from a distant waterfall.

In awe, I climbed a rock to take it in, only to realize I couldn't see the king's hut anywhere. Then a shadow moved between the trees. My heart clenched.

A roar split the air. Gugu froze as a man crouched behind her rose to full height. His voice shook the earth, more beast than human. She fainted on the spot.

"Nkanyamba! It's me—Mpande! Remember?" I shouted, clutching her in my arms.

The man faltered, confusion flashing in his eyes. But before I could move, a figure in a black robe appeared behind me.

"Sleep," the stranger commanded.

Darkness swallowed me.

When I awoke, dizziness clouded my head. Warriors surrounded us. Gugu lay nearby, still as stone.

A man knelt beside me, pressing a clay pot into my hands. "Drink this."

"Is she all right?" I asked, panicked.

"She will be. But both of you must drink."

I obeyed, and they raised Gugu to sip as well. She coughed, then stirred. Strength surged through me as the drink spread through my veins.

"What do you remember?" the man asked.

Gugu blinked in confusion. "We only walked into the bushes for air…"

I echoed her words, and we were led back to the great harvest.

The king was still seated, laughter echoing from his court. The warriors whispered to him, and he listened with a hand on his chin. After a pause, he laughed softly and shook his head.

"Fascinating," he murmured.

Then, louder: "Nkosi, my friend, how are you?"

I turned. My father stood behind me. He bowed lightly. "Ndabezitha, I am well, grateful for life. I pray we've caused no trouble."

"None," said the king. "Children wander. That is their way. Nothing sinister here."

"With your permission, we'll return to the others. I left Nhlanhla worried, and this one must spend time with his uncle before he returns to the Swati lands."

"Of course. You need no permission—you are among your own." The king smiled, then added, "But one thing, Nkosi:

your boy should spend less time chasing girls. I'll have my son Khaya be his companion."

My father placed a hand on my shoulder and bowed. "Very well."

We re-joined the family. Gugu was escorted away, eyes lowered, and I felt a knot of worry tighten in my chest.

Nhlanhla embraced me, checking me over. "What happened?" she whispered.

"He's made a royal friend," my father said, settling beside my uncle.

"What have you gotten yourself into?" my uncle muttered with a little laugh.

I stayed silent, unsure if he meant it for me or himself.

As I ate, my father leaned close. "Well, son. Your life will never be the same."

Before I could ask what he meant, a man's booming voice cut through the evening. "Nkosi!"

A large-bellied man stormed forward, his wife and Gugu trailing behind.

"Keep this monster away from my daughter!" he bellowed.

Fear crawled up my spine. Nhlanhla wrapped her arms around me.

"Are you here to talk," my father asked calmly, "or to fight? Your fists are already clenched."

Sweat trickled down the man's face. His wife stepped forward, voice sharp. "Your son broke my boy's hand, and now he shames my daughter! This dog of yours needs training."

My father stood, no cane needed, and jabbed a finger at the man's face. "Call my son a dog again, and I'll hand him sticks and let him thrash you as he did your foolish boy. At least now I know where that stupidity came from."

My uncle hid a grin, covering his face.

"Leave," my father hissed. "Or stay, and test him yourself."

The woman dragged her husband away. "This is not over!" she spat.

Gugu kept her eyes down as she followed.

"Well, that went well," my uncle chuckled.

I curled deeper into Nhlanhla's embrace.

"Could he beat him?" my uncle asked, lifting his gourd of beer.

My father smiled. "He beat ten boys his age without taking a single blow."

Shock shot through me. How did he know? I had told no one.

My uncle eyed me, a wicked grin spreading across his face. "A little monster indeed. But then, so are we."

Nhlanhla stroked my hair. "Pay no mind, child."

"Nkosi," my uncle pressed, "I want to see it tomorrow before I leave. Let him join us. Is he like me?"

"You wish," my father laughed, tears in his eyes.

The night ended in songs, gifts, and laughter as we packed to leave. My uncle sang horribly with a horn of beer in hand, my father puffed his pipe, and together they stumbled home, the two of them roaring with joy into the night.

Chapter 9

My father woke me earlier than usual. I was still deep in sleep; my eyes felt like heavy stones, reluctant to open. It was dark outside, and I swore he had never slept a wink to wake me at this hour. "Time to go," he whispered.

I groaned but hardly protested. Together, we stepped into the darkness of the jungle. The sounds of owls and crickets filled the air, and the stars scattered like diamonds across the sky while the moon shone bright above. We climbed a mountain and eventually stopped at a clearing.

My uncle dropped a small sack and knelt, burning something as smoke curled from the ground. "What is he doing?" I asked.

"He's laying a shield around us. It'll only take a few minutes," my father replied.

I saw nothing and chose to stay quiet, waiting to see what would happen. Minutes later, my uncle stood, stretching, then removed his robe and looked at us.

"Who's first?" he asked.

"All yours," my father said, pointing at me. Confused, I glanced down; I was the only one carrying sticks.

"Go at him with everything you've got. Don't hold back," my father said, stepping back to sit on a fallen tree trunk.

"Where are your sticks?" I asked, baffled.

"Do not worry, young one. I won't break those little ones you have. Now, let's begin."

He charged.

"Wait!" I yelled, stepping back.

"What now?" he asked, irritation creeping into his tone.

I looked at my father, but he sat in silence. "Aren't there any rules?"

"There are no rules in a fight," my uncle barked. "You just fight. Nothing prepares you for it, so stop fooling around!" His expression was fierce, and I wasn't ready.

He charged again. I hesitated, swinging my stick but missing. He blocked it with his bare hand and punched my chest, knocking me off balance.

"You hesitated. Do not hold back!" he yelled.

I lunged forward, unsure of myself. I had never seen him like this, and it scared me. I aimed for his shoulders, but he avoided every strike. Then he held up his hand, signalling me to stop.

He walked to a nearby tree, broke off a branch, stripped it clean of leaves, and returned. "I hope this will make it easier. Let's try again."

I attacked harder, knowing he now had a weapon. The first blow hit my cheek, stinging sharply. He retaliated with the branch to my chest, driving the pain through me—but I kept fighting. We exchanged blows, each of us landing a lucky hit here and there, though I knew he let me connect just to teach me.

I focused, pouring everything into my attacks. He was faster than my father, but I learned his movements, his shifting positions, and adjusted. Yet, no weakness appeared in his technique. Exhaustion clawed at me, and I wished I could stop—but then he struck the back of my head and kicked me. Fury surged through me.

I turned, pouring all my strength into every blow, moving faster, striking harder. "Now you're fighting, not thinking!" he mocked.

A force hurled me across the clearing. Dust rose, but I got up, fists clenched. My sticks were in his hands.

"Enough," he said, walking toward me. He smiled, patted my shoulder, and sat beside my father.

"He still needs more time," my uncle said.

I collapsed on the ground, body aching. My father handed me water, followed by a fruit.

"I saw what you meant, Nkosi," my uncle said. "But he has no idea what he's doing."

"I know," my father replied. "We were going to start training after the harvest."

"You mean after a week of sleep?" my uncle scoffed.

"Do not rush progress. The body needs rest. He should have connected with himself first, before fighting."

"Nonsense," my uncle said. "They threw sticks at me and told me to fight. You're being soft."

I sat quietly, bored by their debate.

"Taking things one step at a time, not forcing results," my father said calmly. My uncle raised his hands in surrender.

"Okay. Pep talk done. Let's train."

My father looked at me softly. "Son, The brain can achieve great things, but when the body dies, it dies too. The spirit alone can live on—sometimes returning in dreams, inhabiting animals, or guiding loved ones. Not every spirit is strong, but ours is. You must learn to use these gifts together: body, brain, spirit."

He paused. "Spell casting uses all three. The brain knows, the spirit fuels, and the body executes."

"That's enough," my uncle interjected, standing. "Your father is just warming you up. You are rare, Nkosi, but weak. Time to train."

Father and uncle squared off, moving like predators in a circle. They exchanged blows—fire and lightning erupting from their forms. I stepped back, awestruck, shielded by invisible walls. The air shimmered with colours, and the battle raged for what felt like half an hour.

Finally, my father helped my uncle to his knees, and a blast of light shot into the air. I watched I shock thinking he killed him but a light covered my uncle.

We ate and rested before heading home as dawn broke. The jungle sang its morning song. My uncle chatted casually, back to his normal self.

As we approached the village, he stopped. "I'm leaving, Nkosi. What happened back there?"

Father looked skyward. "I don't know... I felt her close by."

My heart jumped. Could my mother still be alive?

Father sighed. "I called out, hoping she would transport me as before, but she only sent healing energy—intended for you."

After bathing, my uncle bid farewell. Not long after, a group entered the yard calling our clan names. The king and his men.

Father and I bowed. The king commanded, "Nkosi, lead us to a place to talk. Your son will come too."

Inside the hut, the air felt heavy. Father offered him a bench; we sat on the floor.

"My son should go to the mountain for initiation," the king began. "It will set him on the path of a man. The Zwane family lodged a complaint—your son fraternizing with their daughter and fighting. This will help him grow."

I froze, stunned.

The king continued. "Gugu is to marry a prince. I'm sorry. But your son and my son will follow the next initiation. It will give him a maternal bond he needs."

Father objected, but the king remained firm. Nhlanhla was brought in. The king asked her, "Will you take Nkosi as your husband?"

"Yes, my king," she said, head bowed.

Father protested; a guard struck him. I leapt, taking up my father's cane, moving with deadly precision. The room froze as the king slammed his spear, shaking the earth.

"Enough!" the king's voice commanded. "This is no child any longer. If you will not take Nhlanhla, I will have her taken elsewhere. Do you understand?"

I froze.

Chapter 10

My father agreed to marry Nhlanhla, and I was set to go to the mountain for initiation a couple of months after my uncle's wedding. Our usual routine continued, though we sometimes spotted a spy when training. The king must have been uneasy after I charged at his guards. We always managed to lose them in the jungle, making sure to set up our protective shield before anyone could see us.

"Today, we will not fight, son," my father said. "Instead, we'll revisit what happened a few days ago. Tell me, what did you see and feel when you charged the king's guard?"

"My mind was blank. I just reacted. But for a moment, I felt everyone's movements inside the room and outside near the door," I replied.

He smiled. "You felt that because your battle cry sent out vibrations—everything it touched came back to you. You'll learn more of that soon."

"Do you believe in magic?" he asked.

"No. I think it's all just tricks to fool people," I answered.

He laughed. "Partly true. But there is real magic. Life, love, and death—it's all magic. You can't see it with your eyes, but it exists. You feel it, and you see it in others without it taking a physical form. It seems normal because everyone wields a bit of it, controls a portion of it. That is what you call magic. There is a way to see it, feel it, and draw strength from it. That's what we will focus on. I want you to see with the sight within."

"But how, Dad?"

"You were born with it, son. We all are. You just have to remember. As children, we rely on our inner sight, but we forget it as we grow, thinking the eyes we see with is everything. Babies are the strongest magic wielders because of their eagerness to learn. The mistake is losing what we already know in the quest for something new and tangible."

We started with breathing techniques, then meditation. Listening became essential—not just to others, but to oneself and the world around. Sometimes we practiced at home, incense burning, clearing our minds. I felt lighter, calmer, and my inner voice spoke more clearly.

"Tell me, what you see?" my father asked, holding out his palm, face up.

I strained, seeing nothing.

"I am holding fire," he said, his hand flicking, "like the kind your uncle produced during our fight—but smaller, beautiful, with splinters of light."

I relaxed, concentrated, and this time, I glimpsed it—tiny sparks dancing above his palm.

"I see it," I whispered.

He laughed, closing his hand. "That was no fire. Only a flash of the lightning I made. A trick, yes—but the fact that you saw something? That is magic." He winked.

Soon, we journeyed to the Swati lands for my uncle's wedding. It took us days, stopping twice in villages to rest. The people welcomed us as guests, offering meals without expecting anything in return. The huts were colourful, with varied shapes unlike the round ones back home.

Dressed in traditional attire adorned with peacock feathers, my father carried his spear; I carried a stick. The wedding ceremony began at the bride's home. We sang cheerful songs as we approached, my grandfather calling out the clan names to seek permission to enter. Elders greeted us, and we stepped inside.

It felt like the harvest all over again—but different. This was not just a union of two people, but of two families. We brought gifts, shared meals, and helped with preparations. A cow was slaughtered, and I assisted in cooking a portion over a small fire as my reward. The rest went to the elders and women. This brought us all together creating a powerful bond between the families.

My father told me I would drink traditional beer only once I became a man. I would join the elders only after marriage. Customs followed; we brought the bride to her new home, covered, signifying marriage. The path was filled with song and celebration, the crowd twice as large as before.

Exhausted after singing, dancing, and participating, we stayed the night at a neighbour's house. The next morning, my uncle guided us only to the king's road, apologizing for not accompanying us further.

"I will be marrying Nhlanhla in a few suns," My father said as we walked.

"It's about time," My uncle said. "You did right by my sister's side, Nkosi. Loss should be met with acceptance, not despair. Life is above all in this plane."

Along the way, we passed a herd of elephants. Majestic, serene, they moved with confidence. "You will see this one day, son," my father whispered. We watched them, connected to nature and the rhythm of life. Giants.

Back home, my father prepared for his wedding, held at the king's court. Almost every villager attended. Beautiful though it was, I felt a tinge of disappointment—I had hoped to see Gugu one last time. Yet, I could not let my feelings overshadow my father's day.

The wedding concluded, and we brought Nhlanhla home, gifts in tow. Cows and goods carried by the king's staff found their places under my father's guidance, Nhlanhla directing the arrangements inside the hut.

As evening fell, my father stepped outside to smoke, and I caught my breath. Nhlanhla sat beside me, silent, thoughtful.

"Mpande, I am not here to replace your mother. God knows she was extraordinary. Your father is remarkable, and you—inside and out—are beautiful. I am honoured to marry into your family. Adjusting won't be easy, but speak freely if anything troubles you. I love you, okay?"

Her sincerity reached me. "I love you too, ma," I replied, wishing I could feel her embrace fully.

She smiled warmly. "Your mother guided me when I was young. I owe her my life, and I would do anything for her. She warned me about marrying a prince who would have been cruel—I ignored her advice at first. But in time, I understood. Now, I'm with your father with his spear and pipe," she whispered, lifting her utensils playfully. I laughed through tears.

Days passed, training continued, and Nhlanhla's warmth made calling her 'mum' feel natural. The virginity testing spectacle arrived; girls sang proudly as they returned. I noticed Gugu with the young prince, laughing among the wealthy elite, and my heart ached. I focused instead on the mountain ahead—the initiation, the transformation.

My father slaughtered a goat and I wore it's skin as a bracelet on my right hand. This meant a lot to me finally finding out my real bloodline, baring my surname and not passed to a family through foster care. Weeks later, I left with other young men. Nhlanhla cried; my father bade me well. The training was harsh, yet fair—every initiate equal. After three months, we returned, transformed into men. Families and other initiates awaited our arrival, praising our journey.

Calling out our clan names, I felt a deep connection:

"Ndlangamandla,
Mphazima, Mntungwa,
Mawandla kaNdlela,
Nina baseMandlovini,
Mlotshwa, Siwela,
Mphazima kaLanga,
Nina bakwaLanga libomvu, elashis'amabel'ezikhuthali,
Mabuya sezembethe'ugogwane,
Mlotshw'akangakanani, ngoba nasentendeni yesandl'uyahlala,
Wena owaphath'induk'emnyama washay'amanzi,
kwavel'udaka,
Nkonjane yenkosi,
Mpangazitha!"

I felt a part of greatness, a Zulu, connected to a lineage that spanned generations. My mother smiled beside my father, tears rolling. A cow was slaughtered in celebration.

The next morning, my father gave me gifts. He showed me a portion of land and a spear crafted by the greatest maker in the land. "This is yours, son. Build your home. Use the weapons to defend, not harm family. You are now a man, but still my son. I love you."

I asked about the king's gift. Respectfully, I declined it—my father had already given me land.

The king explained that as a man, I could not sleep in my father's hut. "Think about it," he said, leaving.

"You should have accepted it to avoid trouble," my father muttered, smiling.

Chapter 11

The hut was truly fit for a king. His majesty had downplayed it, for he never mentioned how vast it really was. The land could have held a small village, complete with its own spring, a flourishing garden, and a kraal kept with care that spoke of years of preparation for a future king.

And now it was mine. Hard to believe, even as I stood within it.

The king entered while I was still admiring the place.
"Do you like it?" he asked.

I turned, bowed. "I love it, my king. Thank you."

He nodded with a smile.

"My king," I said with confidence, "I would like to serve under your warriors, with your permission. I am a good fighter, and I believe I am ready."

The king chuckled, stepping close and laying a hand on my shoulder.
"What is the rush, son? There is much ahead of you. You still have to find yourself a wife among these beautiful young women. This place is far too large for you to live in alone with only helpers. Don't you think?"

"Helpers?" I asked, confused.

"Oh yes. You will need them. Do you imagine you can herd cattle, work the gardens, clean, cook, and still train with your father in the Spear Mountains? No, my son."

I frowned, but he explained further as we sat together.
"Look. You already own wealth men twice your age wish they had. Wealth grows if it is cared for. The boy tending your herd

is the second son in a family of five — his inheritance will be little. You will give him two cows and a sheep as payment. Any calves and lambs born will be his, and he will keep them in your kraal. By the time he reaches your age, he will be as well-off as you. The helpers in your household will share from the garden, trading for what they need. This house runs itself."

I understood, though my heart still longed for the warriors' ranks rather than marriage or household affairs. There was only one way to prove myself ready: the Village Challenge.

I trained with my father until that day.

The field lay open between the King of Kings' great city and the mountains. Men from every village gathered spears in hand. We hurled them at one another as sport — not to kill, though if a man fell, blame was cast on witchcraft or blindness. Some tested their skill by catching spears before they struck the ground. One spear, however, soared higher than the rest, plunging deep into the earth with such force that none dared touch it. Whispers ran through the men — they all knew whose spear it was.

When all spears were collected, we gathered at the field's centre. Each man had two choices: lift a spear and challenge its owner, or pick a man from the crowd. Most spears bore marks or carvings. We mocked, we boasted, we greeted each other like brothers and rivals alike.

The kings stood apart, speaking among themselves. I kept scanning the crowd. Today I would carve my name into memory.

The horn sounded. From the far side of the field, giants appeared — four of them, larger than the one I had seen at the harvest. They led fifty fierce warriors each, and in their midst walked the King of Kings himself.

His robe was woven of gold, and a lion's head crowned him. A golden spear rested in his left hand. Every step his giants took made the ground tremble. We bowed, even from a distance. The energy he carried was suffocating — overwhelming — as though a shield of power radiated from him.

His praise singer's voice thundered, and only when it was done did we dare rise. He spoke briefly, then sat in full view of the field. At his signal, the challenges began.

Ten men stepped forward, pairs colliding with roars and flashing spears. I pushed through the crowd, eager to be closer. The fighters were skilled, but none matched my father. I studied them, hungry for a worthy opponent.

Beside me stood a man from the mountain. "I thought you had run. Are you ready for your first fight as a man?" he asked.

I smirked. "You cannot challenge me. We are on the same side, remember?"

"Then whose spear did you pick?" he pressed.

"You'll find out when I call my challenge," I said with a wink.

Then the crowd stirred. A man stepped out from the other side, greeted by thunderous cheers. His name was whispered like a curse.

"Mandla," the man beside me muttered. "From the King's city. He fought once, and since then none of the thirteen clans have dared face him."

Mandla raised his arms as if already victorious. His grin split wide as he called, "Did anyone catch my spear?"

The crowd laughed. "No one ever has," my companion whispered. "It stays buried in the earth. After his show, he will fetch it himself and sit beside the king, as he has for two years."

But this time, I stepped out holding that very spear.

The crowd gasped.

"Well," I said, ". Mandla shook his head. Laughter rippled through the men.

I stepped forward. A hand gripped my arm. "Is this a death wish, boy?" the man hissed.

I shook free, eyes burning. "I am no boy."

I lifted the spear high. Silence fell. My king's voice called my name in alarm. I glanced at him — he stood pacing near the King of Kings. But there was no turning back.

"I accept the challenge!" I declared.

Mandla burst out laughing. "That is not my spear, young man."

I hurled it to him. He caught it with ease, examined it, and his face darkened. "Impossible. Who helped you pull it out?"

"Enough talk. Do you accept, or?"

The crowd roared when he stepped forward. I armed myself with another spear. The duel began.

Mandla was strong, his movements fast, his strikes like a mamba. But I had the technique passed down by those who once guarded the King of Kings himself. I struck with precision, forcing him back. When I disarmed him, the crowd erupted.

I cast aside my spear. We fought hand-to-hand, blows heavy and fast. He nearly floored me with his strength, but I kept distance, darting in and out, striking where it hurt most, and waiting for him to tire.

Finally, I brought him to one knee.

I leapt to finish it — but he snatched a spear and thrust for my heart. In mid-air, I twisted, locking the weapon between my ribs and arm, wrenching it from his grip. My left fist landed clean across his jaw.

He fell.

I stood ready. He rose slowly, and then lifted his hands in surrender. I stepped close and offered my hand. We clasped arms, and the field shook with cheers.

"I nearly killed you," Mandla said, regret plain.

"Do not worry. Thank you for not holding back," I replied.

My king reached me through the celebrating crowd. "You are as crazy as your father, Mpande," he said, clasping my hand. "Give this man a mixture of herbs for his wound!"

The cut near my ribs healed quickly. But nothing healed as fast as the bond I had just made with the crowd, and with destiny itself.

From there, life changed. I joined the Hyena Group under Bongani Ntuli, who refused promotion so his men could rise with him. We trained, fought, hunted — brothers bound not by blood, but by choice. Around them, I was free. They kept my secret — that I could cast while fighting.

Bongani, my sparring partner, earned my respect. His strength was nothing compared to his mind — sharp, calm, able to make the complex simple. With him, I pushed limits. colours appeared when I fought, flames and lightning sometimes flashing from my sticks. I learned to channel energy, striking even without contact.

My home stood grand, yet empty. My heart felt fuller in the wild with my brothers.

Months later, I returned home. My mother was pregnant, my father growing a belly of his own. They welcomed me with food and laughter. My father already knew of my fight — news travelled fast.

We trained together, his strength undiminished. "You cannot beat me with that belly," I teased.

"Boy," he said, laughing, "there is power in marriage. Everything grows including this bag of traditional beer and home cooked meals. You will see when you find a wife."

I laughed it off, though his words lingered.

The days dragged on, each moment stretched by the heaviness of what I carried inside. My father's words echoed in my head, his scorn still burning in my chest. I tried to drown it out with work, but even the cattle seemed to sense my unrest. They shifted uneasily, lowing as if unsettled by the storm within me.

When the sun finally dipped and the shadows lengthened across the land, I felt the pull again—stronger than before. It wasn't the restless kind of anger or despair. No, this was different. It was steady, insistent, like a hand guiding me toward something I could neither name nor resist.

I found myself drawn to the mountain once more. The sky above was painted in bruised purples and fading gold. My feet knew the path before my mind did. Each step away from home lightened my spirit, even as dread gnawed at the edges of my resolve.

The river roared in the distance, its voice louder than I remembered, as though calling to me alone. By the time I reached its edge, darkness had settled, and the moon's pale glow shimmered across the rushing water.

I stood there, trembling—not from fear, but from the weight of the moment. And yet, beneath it all, there was that warmth again. That unseen presence, which once prevented me from giving up entirely. I closed my eyes. I heard it.

"Mpande," it whispered, steady as the river. "Your life is not meant for despair. What you carry is greater than pain. You will suffer, yes. But you will also rise. This path is not chosen by chance. Do not run from it—walk it."

I knelt at the water's edge, the soil damp beneath my knees, and for the first time, I did not feel alone.

I stood my body weary but my spirit steadier than before. With one last look at the river, I turned toward the path home, each step lighter, though the weight of what awaited me still lingered. For the first time, I felt I could carry it.

Not long after, word came: the King of Kings summoned me. Nine warriors were sent to escort me. None knew why.

On the road, we met a madman who shouted riddles at me: "What a waste of talent! What have you learnt, son of the mighty Nguni, sticks and stones?" His words haunted me as we camped that night.

I could not sleep. With spear in hand, I wandered into the darkness. A branch snapped — footsteps fled. I pursued, but a figure dropped from the trees.

"Back, Mpande," he ordered. "We must leave this place."

I obeyed, though I wondered how he knew my name. His words soon revealed the truth: the resistance was near, their assassins trained and ready. We rushed to warn the king.

That night, as we caught our breath, a woman's voice filled my mind: "Form a circle. I will shield you. Place Mpande on Lukhanyo's left."

I froze. "Who is Lukhanyo?"

The youngest of our group looked at me, startled. I knew then. I moved beside him.

"You can hear her?" Sabelo Langa, the man from earlier, asked quietly. I nodded.

A shadow streaked overhead. Then riders burst from the clearing — horses, beasts I had only heard of. On them sat men clad in black leather, armed with sharp foreign weapons.

And at their head, a white man. Umlungu. His uniform was royal blue trimmed with gold, his sword gleaming at his side. His eyes burned with fury as he dismounted, scanning the night.

"Find them!" he commanded in a tongue I somehow understood. "We cannot fight the King's army so hunt them all. Kill them before they reach the city."

His men scattered, leaving him alone.

He turned, hand resting on the hilt of his massive blade, eyes narrowing as he stepped toward us.

My palms slicked with sweat around my spear. My heart thundered.

And I knew: the real challenge had only just begun.

.

Chapter 12

The white man unbuckled his pants to urinate.

"Let us kill this thing before the others get back," one of the escorts whispered.

"As long as they do not see us, we will be fine. We will move silently as soon as he leaves. We are not far from the next village," Sabelo answered.

The man mounted his horse again and rode off. The shield around us faded, and we began to move carefully through the jungle, heading for the next village. A shadow swept across our heads once more, and though we could not see what it was, every part of me knew it was nothing good.

Then, a figure dropped from the sky, landing before us.

We froze. My body stiffened in fear as the figure slowly rose.

"I think I am getting accustomed to men falling from the sky," I muttered, eyes fixed on the shape before us. "But what puzzles me is that there are no trees ahead."

"That is no man. We are screwed," Sabelo said, and though it was dark, I could see sweat glistening on his brow.

"We might be able to go back and try to lose this thing in the jungle, but I'm afraid we—"

Before Sabelo could finish, a horse thundered behind us. I heard a sound like an axe striking wood. Then a head rolled across the ground.

I realized only as the rider passed us that he had cut down one of the escorts with a single, clean swing of his sword.

Nothing prepares you for such a sight. No training steels you against the face of death. My hands weakened, and my spear slipped from my grasp.

The other three horsemen appeared, flanking the swordsman.

Sabelo bent, picked up my spear, and pressed it back into my hands. I met his eyes with a blank stare, my mind too stunned for words.

He stepped forward, his voice rising with fury. "Who are we?"

"We are Zulu!" the escorts roared in unison.

They repeated it, and this time, I joined, the strength of their voices pouring into me.

"The body dies so the earth, animals may feed and live. The spirit will live forever. Who are we?!" Sabelo cried, advancing another step.

"We are Zulu!" we answered.

"We are of God. Let us rain thunder on them!"

With battle cries splitting the night, we charged forward. One of the escorts hurled his spear, and it tore through one of the horsemen, hurling him off his mount.

We pressed on, but when another escort cast his spear, a glowing shield shimmered into existence and blocked it.

The horses reared and halted on the far side of the barrier. The riders dismounted. Our charge slowed, doubt flickering in our steps.

The escort who had thrown his spear sprinted forward to reclaim it. The shield opened with a sudden pulse, followed by a deafening bang. Smoke burst from a gun, and the man fell where he crouched, lifeless.

When I lifted my head, I saw the white man aiming a rifle at Sabelo.

I lunged, shoving him aside. Another blast tore the air. The bullet grazed me, hot and sharp.

Fury overtook me. I sprang to my feet and charged the horsemen with a roar, spear raised. They scrambled, trying to reload, but I reached them first.

One swung his sword. I parried blow after blow, then thrust my spear into his gut. His body collapsed to its knees, and I froze, chest heaving, staring.

Had I just killed a man?

A spear whistled past, snapping me out of my trance. The white man blocked it with ease, his sword flashing. He turned, pointing the blade toward the dark figure cloaked in black behind him.

Confusion twisted in me—until Sabelo shouted, "Get down!"

I dropped instantly. A white flash tore across the air, heat rushing over me, the energy searing even above my head.

The white man advanced, his sword raised. He swung, and the force shattered my spear in two. I clenched the broken halves, turning them into fighting sticks, circling, staying out of reach of that massive blade. If I could tire him out, perhaps I could strike.

Behind me, the others managed to slay the last of the horsemen. The white man glanced over his shoulder, panic flickering across his face.

"What the hell is taking so long, witch!?" he barked.

"It is no small magic, you fool," the dark figure hissed. "Keep them off me—especially that one. His magic is everywhere!"

I knew what I had to do—fight, distract, and endure. Sabelo and the others joined me, but the witch raised another barrier, trapping us outside.

"What are they doing?" I growled in frustration.

The white man began calmly reloading his rifle, his sinister smile gleaming through the barrier.

"We have to fall back, take cover. If that shield opens and he fires again, one of us will surely die," I said.

Sabelo's face hardened. "I have an idea, though it is not a good one. Turning back is no option. We will run into an army. Instead—we ask for a shield of our own. One strong enough to block whatever this white witch is conjuring. My lady—are you listening?" he called to the sky.

Silence.

He looked at me, sadness in his eyes. "We are left with no choice. Let us run. Not back, but along this shield's edge. If they want to stop us, it must be from reaching the city."

The men hesitated. I stepped forward. "We are not cowards, but we are no fools either. Let us live to fight another day."

We ran to the right, keeping the youngest in the middle in case a shot rang out. Sabelo kept pressing against the barrier, searching for an end.

Then, the air cracked with thunder. A blinding flash lit the sky.

From it emerged a beast—massive, striped like a tiger, maned like a lion, its roar shaking the ground.

The barrier shimmered, and then fell away.

Sabelo let out a laugh that chilled me. "There is no escaping that. It must have drained the witch to summon it. And she is not working alone."

"What is that?" I whispered.

"That is a Lyga. A lion-tiger hybrid, once guardian to an Egyptian priestess. They said it was a myth. This creature once slaughtered half of the Zulu Hundred before falling."

The witch lifted her hands, pointing directly at us. The Lyga's roar rattled my bones. My mind emptied. Then—clarity struck.

Colours radiated from the beast—blood red, white, purple. I looked skyward, and a rainbow of light seemed to rain upon me.

Energy surged in my chest like a drumbeat. Chants filled my ears.

"Mpande!" Sabelo shouted.

I turned, a shield forming around me. I only nodded, then charged.

My feet pounded, fists clenched, speed rising as the Lyga leapt.

"Mpande!" a woman's voice called from above.

The voice inside me urged: *Now.*

I saw it—the black void in the Lyga's chest. With a scream, I hurled myself into it. My spear pierced its spine. I burst through its thick hide, emerging atop the beast's back, roaring.

I turned toward the witch and the white man, their faces stricken with disbelief. The same colours that had radiated from the Lyga burned within her.

The sky answered with a roar. Lightning split the clouds, and Nkhanyamba descended—a serpent of storm and cloud, its tail whipping across the heavens. He struck at the witch, but she tore open a portal, vanishing with the white man before his blow could land.

Nkhanyamba landed beside me. "They are not meant to see me," he said. "They might die. We will speak when you return."

With that, he leapt skyward, tail thrashing, and disappeared into the clouds. The storm subsided, leaving only rain.

The barrier around Sabelo and the others dissolved. They stared at me, mouths open.

"Let us head to the city," I said, though unknowingly pointing the wrong way.

Sabelo laughed, correcting me, and we began our journey.

It took two days to reach the city, stopping to bathe in the valleys and rest in villages where the Nguni people welcomed us as though we were kings.

By the time we arrived, night had fallen. I was taken to the king's hut. Sabelo smiled wide. "I owe you a great deal, Mpande. Tomorrow, you will meet my family."

That night, I feasted; bathed, and slept in the softest covers I had ever known.

At dawn, roosters woke me. Unlike Johannesburg, the air here was alive with nature—birds, cattle, voices of life.

Two young women entered, carrying fine leather clothes and a clay pot of water. They instructed me to bathe near the fire, then join the King of Kings in the great hall.

When I entered, the hall erupted in cheers. Men shouted my name until the King of Kings struck his spear twice against the floor. Silence fell, an opening formed, and I walked forward.

A man stepped before me, declaring:

"Mpande! Son of Nkosi, breaker of bones, slayer of the Lyga, the first of his kind!"

The hall roared again, but the King of Kings rose, arms open, and embraced me. He seated me at his right hand, beside his eldest son.

"This is not celebration," he said. "We still march against an enemy that plots to destroy the royal line."

I soon learned that the youngest prince himself had been one of my escorts. No wonder the witch had tried so desperately to end us.

I volunteered at once to join the war party.

Later, Sabelo led me to his hut. His wife turned, smiling.

"Mpande. Slayer of the Lyga. Soon-to-be king. How are you?"

My heart froze.

Sabelo kissed her cheek, beaming. "Mpande, this is my family."

I bowed slightly. "Gugu."

"You know each other?" Sabelo asked, puzzled.

"We come from the same village," she said lightly. Then, with a smile, "And now I—am the greatest White Witch the Nguni nation has ever known."

The words left me stunned. "I thought White witches were white people like the ones we met at the jungle, you know different skin tone?" I asked puzzled and they both laughed hard.

Over breakfast, I pressed her for truth. She told me of her blooming powers, of the queen's schemes, of betrayal and escape.

I listened in silence. She healed the sick before my eyes, scolding me gently. "There is more to life than fighting, Mpande. Perhaps in giving life, you too will find peace."

Her words cut deep.

Sabelo returned. "We march soon."

We left the hut, joining the war party. I was placed at the front with the princes.

Voices lifted in songs of war, feet stamping the earth.

The march to destiny had begun.

Chapter 13

The battle erupted in the heart of the jungle before midday. What surprised me most was that we were not just fighting outsiders— some of our opponents were Nguni clans, including Zulu warriors, and a few foreigners no more than fifty. Blood soaked the ground, and I saw neither honor nor glory in this chaos. Every life taken, even in battle, felt like a weight on my soul. I nearly lost myself to despair, and it was only Sabelo's presence that kept me alive. Sabelo moved with lethal precision. The Langa people drew strength from the Sun, and the fire he radiated in battle was unstoppable. Slowly, our enemies fell, bodies piling up around us. The sight made me sick, nearly to the point of vomiting. But then the White Witch appeared. Everything went haywire. Animals under her spell attacked our men from the sides. Gunshots rang through the jungle, cutting down warriors in front of me. Rage surged, transforming my despair into unstoppable energy. I attacked with a newfound ferocity, and our warriors' morale soared. Zulu battle cries echoed like thunder, filling the air with the rhythm of war. I struck a shield while fending off men on all sides. I tried desperately not to kill, only to wound—but the battlefield demanded more. I looked to the sky and roared, piercing the shield as I had pierced the Lyga. Warriors pressed on, some banging on from the other side, but it was safer for them to remain there. The Witch's power was too dangerous. The White man with the massive sword appeared behind her. I gripped my spear tightly, poured every ounce of energy into it, and let it fly. It hit its mark squarely in her shoulder. The Witch's scream pierced the air, a sound that chilled every bone. That should keep her from causing more havoc.

Meanwhile in Mpande's original timeline

The council chamber smelled of polish and perfume; a thin, civilized air that tried — uselessly — to hide the rot beneath. Men in tailored suits tugged at collars and shifted in leather chairs while the Witch's sisters stood back in the shadowed doorway, beads tick-clicking like a slow, mechanical heartbeat.

The White Witch in a grey suit set the badge on the table with more care than one would place a weapon. The gold ate the light; the blood darkened like ink spreading across a page.

"This is the boy," she said. The voice was silk pulled tight over a blade. "Taste."

An elder — a minister whose hands trembled when he signed papers but never when he led prayers — took the badge to his lips. For a heartbeat his face opened as if an old wound had been unearthed. Memory crawled up, claws slick with earth. The circle stirred a low rustle of disbelief.

"Impossible," someone breathed. "That line— it was broken."

"Clearly not," she replied, smiling as a woman might smile at a closed door. "He lives. If he rises, everything we have built here collapses. Our gates open; our names die in the mouths of children. Do you understand what that means?"

A younger councillor leaned forward until his voice became a hiss. "So what do you propose?"

The Witch's smile thinned until it was only intent. "We shackle him," she said, each word measured. "We draw blood from his veins until the key is stained. We lock the secret away. Or — if the door remembers and shows mercy — we kill the memory before it is given a name."

Silence closed around the table like a lid. No one laughed. No one mocked. The smell of perfume seemed suddenly cloying, the polish too bright.

An older man, his face mapped with ledger lines and lost alliances, rubbed the badge between thumb and forefinger and then, almost gently, said, "Fine. Prepare the chains. Find the old rites. If we must bleed a future to keep our past, then so be it."

The sisters' beads chimed once. The decision settled like snow — quiet, inevitable — and the room returned to business as if nothing had happened at all.

I heard the army roar behind me as the shield began to crumble. I stepped forward toward the White man and the Witch, now sobbing on the ground, ready for the fight I knew was inevitable. Lightning streaked across the sky in broad daylight, though no rain fell. Before I could react, a powerful force blasted me to the portion of the shield that was still up, and I hit hard, vision blurred. colours swirled before my eyes, pain searing through me, evoking that familiar, helpless feeling from before. I touched the back of my head, tasted blood, and laughed. Zulu people are said to have hard heads, after all. The Witch's figure, standing tall despite her injury, glowed with power. "You," she hissed, "I am starting to hate you, and it's high time I put an end to this." With a twist of her fingers, I felt my back bend as if I were to break in two Pains like no other consumed me. For the first time, I felt utterly powerless. My mind wandered to Jasmine, her big, warm eyes comforting me, and strangely, I found peace in that fleeting thought. "Even when you can't move forward, Mpande," she once told me with that half-smile of hers, "you can still choose not to fall back." Tears fell freely. Death didn't scare me—I could surrender to it. "No! You will not slip away so easily," the Witch shrieked as if we said it in unison. "This was not to kill you—yet. It was to paralyze you, to watch helplessly as your brethren burn." I want you to feel the pain I felt when you took my child". Oh the Lyga. "I wanted to study you… but perhaps death is better. Now, watch!" Lightning struck indiscriminately, frying warriors before my eyes. Chaos screams, and fire surrounded me. I tried to close my eyes, but I could not escape the horror. "Enough!" I screamed. I willed movement into my limbs. Hands shaking, I reached for the sky, gathering life itself into my being. I kicked; my body vibrating with energy, then brought my leg down with earth-shaking force. Step by step, motion by motion, I shattered the Witch's spell. I drew energy from the life around me, a bit from the sun above, the ground beneath, ancestors, until I felt unstoppable. When I struck the Witch with a final, concentrated release of power, a flash of light erupted, a cannon-like boom tearing through the jungle. Dust filled the air. The shield behind me vanished. Cheers erupted from our men. Sabelo's warm hand rested on my shoulder. "You have to tell me how you killed a witch with just a dance," he said, disbelief thick in his voice. "If you teach me how to draw strength from the sun," I said, laughing, "I'll teach you how to dance." Sabelo smirked. "For that, my friend, I'd have to marry you as a second wife," he joked, and we both laughed. The Zulu dance was actually a dance of power.

A small light flickered in the dust. The Witch screamed in fury. A white beam shot out, and the White man readied his attack. "Gugu!" Sabelo called, and she appeared, creating a shield that shimmered as it absorbed the force. Then she levitated, hurling a ball of fire that grew to the size of a small sun. The Witch's scream echoed as she vanished. Gugu landed gracefully, dusting her robe. "Look at this mess," she said. "Some need to be carried home. I'll deal with the severely injured. Using this much energy is dangerous, Mpande—move!"

We obeyed, helping the wounded back to the city. Along the way, Sabelo explained how he channelled inner strength, mixing it with life's elements, with the Sun as the most potent source.

The king of kings welcomed us back, grateful for our survival. He offered a celebration, even land, livestock, and the pick of wives among his people. "My king," I said, bowing, "we fought brothers today. There is no victory here. Let us honour our fallen and help their families. I also wish to travel among the clans, even outside the Zulu kingdom, to unite our people, to understand this division and forge a lasting union." The king paused but eventually nodded. "I will support you. Take my best men and a White Witch to guide you."

I met the companions: five men and two women. Among them were Leo, a man of mixed heritage whose father had been stranded here, Thando and Martha, the White Witch who had trained Gugu and saved her from certain death. Our journey was long and hard, filled with skirmishes, learning, and diplomacy. Martha trained me in herbs, spells, and healing. Thando, though wary of Martha, watched over me fiercely. Over time, I began to see Martha differently—her care, her gentleness, her simplicity.

She became someone I admired, and we shared long walks and conversations. "Martha," I asked once, away from the others, "what did you do to Thando?" "Nothing," she said, eyes wide. "Don't act surprised. I saw you cast a spell." "It didn't work," Martha replied, bored. "Why, does she have some secret ability?" I said, confused. "No, She has the strongest magic of all: love," Martha said, matter-of-factly. I froze. "She loves you, stupid. That's why my spell failed." I couldn't respond. She smiled. Then she asked, gently, without looking at me "What about Jasmine?"

Chapter 14

Martha's voice cut through the night air like a blade.
"What about Jasmine?"

The name hit me harder than any spear. My body stiffened the
question lodging deep in my chest.

I turned slowly, meeting Martha's eyes. There was fire there,
but beneath it, something wounded. "What about her?" I asked,
though my throat tightened at the sound of her name.

Martha stepped closer, her jaw tense. "Don't play games with
me, Mpande. You know what I mean. Even in death, she clings
to you. I've seen it. The way your spirit bends toward her
whenever she crosses your mind."

I swallowed hard. Images of Jasmine's eyes—warm, alive—
rose before me, steadying me in ways I never admitted. A
memory surfaced unbidden:

*"Mpande," Jasmine once told me, laughing at my silence, "you
brood too much. But I love that about you—it means you carry
people inside your heart, even when it hurts you."*

Hearing her voice in my mind felt like balm and salt all at once.

"Martha," I whispered, "it's not what you think. Jasmine is…
was… different."

Martha's breath hitched, her lips pressing into a hard line.
"Different? She's gone, Mpande. And yet she lives in your
every pause, in the way you flinch when you think no one
notices. You carry her like a ghost, while I—" She broke off,
blinking back the wetness in her eyes.

I stepped forward, wanting to reach for her, but my hands fell uselessly at my sides. "You're here. You've stood by me when others would have walked away. That is something worth holding on to, Martha."

Her laugh was sharp, bitter. "Something worth holding on to you say? Do you hear yourself? I'm flesh and blood, Mpande. I've bled for you, fought beside you. Yet I will never be enough, will I? Not while the shadow of Jasmine's love lingers over us both."

The silence that followed pressed on my chest like a weight. I wanted to argue, to tell her she was wrong. But the truth burned too close to the surface.

I lowered my gaze. "I never asked for this war inside me," I said quietly. "But I can't deny it either. Jasmine… she reminds me of who I once was. You remind me of who I wanted to be."

Martha's shoulders slumped, anger giving way to exhaustion. She shook her head. "Then maybe you don't see me at all."

Her words cut deeper than any witch's curse.

The fire between us dimmed to embers. I felt smaller than I had ever felt in battle, as though stripped bare.

For the first time since this fight began, I wondered not just about victory or survival, but about love—and whether it could truly endure in a world torn apart by shadows and blood.

I lifted my eyes to the horizon, where the stars blinked faintly. A thousand destinies seemed to hang there, waiting. Yet in that moment, I had never felt more lost.

The Gathering Flame

The night fires burned bright, painting faces in gold and shadow. Tribes from across the land had gathered—Zulu, Sotho, Tswana, and many more—each carrying their scars, each wary of the other. Old grudges whispered between the cracks, but tonight, they stood shoulder to shoulder. With Jasmine in mind I knew how the future looked and this might be a way to prevent my people from suffering.

Drums pulsed steady, a heartbeat calling them into something greater than themselves.

I stood with Lethabo at the edge of the circle. His jaw was set, eyes scanning the crowd, shoulders tense as though carrying the weight of every soul present. He had called them here, after all. This was his moment to unite what had always been divided.

But before the speeches, the pledges, and the oaths, there was life—raw, unfiltered.

Children laughed as they chased one another between the legs of warriors. Women clapped along to the drums, voices rising like smoke into the sky. And in the middle of it all, I saw her— Divashni.

Her laughter was a melody above the beat of the drums. She moved with the rhythm, her bracelets clinking as she spun, sari edges catching the firelight. People watched her—Zulu, Tsonga, Venda—and for once, no one measured her by the tone of her skin or the lineage of her ancestors.

She belonged here. Completely.

A boy too small to dance on his own tugged at her hand, and she scooped him up, spinning him as he squealed. An elder clapped approval, smiling despite the years of bitterness etched into his face.

I caught a fragment of her voice as she leaned down to the child, words that drifted toward me on the fire lit air: *"Different colours, different songs—but all of us carry the same heart. Do you feel it? Listen... the drums don't care what tongue you speak."*

Her joy was contagious. Even hardened warriors softened, tapping their spears to the earth in time with her laughter.

For a moment, the gathering felt less like a council of tribes preparing for war and more like a family rediscovering itself.

And then the mood shifted.
One of the younger warriors, eager and restless, struck his spear into the ground. "Words and songs are fine," he called, "but what of strength? Who among us can fight when the enemy comes?"

All eyes turned. Divashni stepped forward.

The firelight caught her face, still glowing with warmth, but now sharpened by resolve. She removed her bracelets, laid the child she had been holding into his mother's arms, and bowed her head briefly.

Then she moved.

Her body flowed like water, yet struck like lightning. Every motion of **Kalari** told a story—low stances that rooted her to the earth, whirling spins that sliced the air, precise strikes that stopped inches from warriors bold enough to step forward and test her. Her hands brushed against pressure points, her kicks snapped with controlled force, and every pivot drew gasps from the crowd.

The ground itself seemed to pulse with her rhythm. She was grace and fury woven together—soft as silk, fierce as fire.

When she finished, her palms pressed together in a bow, sweat glistening at her brow. The warriors she had faced stepped back, their eyes lit not with resentment, but with respect.

The tribes erupted in cheers. Children mimicked her moves, elders nodded with approval, and even the doubters who had whispered now fell silent.

Divashni returned to her place quietly, smile returning as though she hadn't just shifted the mood of the entire gathering. She was more than a warrior; she was proof that belonging meant more than blood or skin—it meant heart and spirit.

Then Lethabo's hand landed on my shoulder. His grip was firm, his face carved from stone. "They're watching me," he muttered. "Waiting to see if I falter."

I glanced at him. "Then don't falter. But don't forget—they're also waiting to see if you trust them. Tonight isn't only about strength, Lethabo. It's about belonging."

His eyes shifted briefly to Divashni, and I saw something soften in him, just for an instant. Then the mask returned, heavy and unyielding.

The drums slowed. The voices quieted. One by one, the tribes turned their eyes to Lethabo, waiting for his words.

The Gathering Flame was his to command. But whether it united or divided us would depend not only on his voice, but on all of us—those who chose to believe in something greater than bloodlines and shadows.

Chapter 15

The group that had gone out to spread word of unity returned two weeks later, dust on their clothes and triumph in their voices. Their news lit a spark in the court: the message had taken root. The tribes would come. The kingdoms would answer. The gathering that was once a whisper on the wind was now a roaring tide.

The King of Kings rose to his feet, his voice filling the hall. "Then it is settled. We will host the greatest gathering in the history of the Nguni people. The drums of unity will echo through these valleys and over these mountains until the stars themselves take notice."

Cheers thundered, warriors striking their spears against the earth, women raising ululations that shook the rafters. I felt the weight of it all sink into my chest. This was no longer talk. This was history being carved into stone.

Thando was at my side, her hand brushing mine, her eyes glowing with quiet pride. She had been my shadow these past weeks, tending to me, preparing meals, soothing my fatigue when the endless meetings drained me. In her presence, I found rest. In her voice, I found calm.

Yet in my heart, there was a silence I could not ignore.

I appreciated her deeply, but it was not the kind of love that scorched through the soul, the kind that Jasmine carried so effortlessly. Thando's love was steady—safe, unwavering, devoted. She spoke of children as though they were already running in our courtyard, of names and futures she could see so clearly. It should have filled me with joy. Instead, it unsettled me.

But I had chosen this path. This life promised stability—
ownership of a household, the honour of marriage, the loyalty
of a people who called me their own. Here, I was not the
outcast. Here, I was a leader.

Back in my original timeline, Jasmine's father had made his
stance clear: I was not welcome near his daughter. My mother,
though smiling now in her marriage, lived a life built on a
different foundation, one where my step father's presence had
shaped my siblings in ways I had never known. I had no place
there, no claim to happiness that was not constantly torn down
by others.

Here, though, I belonged. I told myself again and again that this
was my life now, and I would live it, no matter what Martha or
anyone else thought. Even if part of me longed for a woman I
could never truly have.

Within two days, I reported everything to the King—the
alliances secured, the plans forged, the enemies still looming.
Martha disappeared into her own silence, Gugu buried herself
in her work, and Sabelo and I only crossed paths in council
chambers. Invitations were dispatched, carried by swift runners
and heralds. One by one, nations answered.

Thando and I were set to be married after the gathering. She
cared for me daily, filling my hut with warmth I had not known
in years. She dreamed aloud of a bright future together. It made
me uneasy, yet I could not deny the comfort she brought to my
weary soul.

This was my life now, were I belonged and I was determined to
see it through—even as I braced for the battles that were surely
coming. For I knew this first victory, this unity, was only the
beginning. The sun was setting, the horizon bathed in a warm
glow that shimmered with a thousand colours. The great city of

the Zulu nation hummed with chatter, yet beneath it all I could still hear the sea whispering in the distance.

I had worked for years to reach this moment, and now the stage was set. Behind me stood giants—icons and leaders with the power to move mountains and change the course of rivers through the sheer force of their influence. Before me stretched a crowd drawn from every corner of this beautiful land, gathered here for one purpose: to hear me speak. The thought alone was astonishing.

I was ready. After all, I had been doing this for some time, and public speaking had never been a weakness of mine. I knew I could command this speech. And yet, today felt different. Beneath my confidence, something stirred—a tremor rising within me that I could not name.

I wore a black and white cotton shirt, soft against my skin, with a V-shaped strip of leopard hide draped over it. My trousers were sleek and slim, designed for comfort by one of our renowned Indian designers. Patiently, I waited for my introduction, still puzzled by his choice of a Zulu crown of cowhide. Yet, as it rested on my head, it felt unexpectedly fitting.

The king, flanked by his five advisors, was delivering a hearty address when the crowd erupted into cheers so thunderous they startled me. The unease within me surged, but I pushed it down, focusing instead on the cool, grounding feel of the wooden stage beneath my bare feet. It was almost comical, considering the mountain of sneakers back in my apartment, yet walking barefoot felt right—natural. I glanced down at the bands woven with red and white beads around my ankles, matched by the ones on my wrists, and smiled.

The cheers faded into a hush. The king stepped aside, leaving the way clear for me. Slowly, I descended the steps, the sea of colour and faces rising into full view. Thousands of eyes fixed on me. I bowed low to the king, and he greeted me with a warm smile before extending his hand. His grip was firm, pulling me into an embrace I never could have imagined. Emotion surged. My eyes burned, tears threatening to fall. I fought them back, but one slipped free, vanishing into the rough of my beard.

When the king released me, he gestured toward the crowd, and I drew a deep breath. But the moment my gaze swept forward, my heart faltered. My throat dried. My eyes locked on a single figure among the masses.

Her.

The feeling surged violently through me. My mouth parted, but no words would come. Before I could speak, the world erupted. Sounds of canon fire filling the air. An explosion thundered from the far left of the city, dust spiralling into the air.

I spun to see the king encircled by his guards, their formation tightening as they moved him back to safety. Women clutched children as they fled, following protocol drilled into them by generations. Shouts of command rang out, the summoning of warriors to arms mixing with the terrified cries of those scattering into the streets. Above the chaos, the deep voices of the Zulu Hundred and the king's guard thundered, strong and steady, assuring me the royal household and the village would soon be secured.

But my eyes dragged back to where they had been—back to her. And in that instant, horror struck.

A spear whistled through the air, screaming toward me with deadly precision. My heart seized. My eyes clamped shut. Darkness consumed me before I could even react. The pain ebbed into nothingness, swallowed by a tide of shadows. My body was heavy, unyielding, yet my spirit drifted free, caught in a current of silence deeper than death itself. I felt myself dissolving, piece by piece, into the vast unknown.

Then—out of that darkness—something stirred. A pull, not of chains, but of light unseen. It was not an end, but a summons. The stars called to me, ancient and patient, their voices threading through the blackness like whispers of destiny.

I closed my eyes to the world I had known, only to open them to the boundless sky above.

Chapter 16

Nkanyezi's voice echoed softly around him as if carried by the wind itself. She wondered aloud why man feared the unknown, when it was within that very darkness that most discoveries lay. Her words hung in the void, settling like warm light over Mpande's spirit. "Who are you?" I asked my voice small in the vastness.

From the darkness, a shimmer gathered—soft, radiant, and endless. It wasn't fire or flesh but something older, something eternal.

"I am Nkanyezi," she said, her tone both gentle and commanding. "The star that has watched over this life and yours is beautiful" the voice marveled.

Her light moved around me like a tide, brushing against the scars of my spirit.

"What do you mean… written?" I whispered.

"This war, these flames, this sorrow—it belongs to this world," she answered, her voice carrying both sorrow and certainty. "But your path does not end here. You must return to your own timeline and write your own story. The lessons you have learned, the battles you have fought—they were to shape you, not to keep you here."

I clenched my fists, anger rising like fire in my chest. "How can I leave? My people are bleeding, dying and I can change things. If I abandon them now, what kind of man does that make me? To fall here, with them, would mean more than running back to a world where none of this matters."

Her glow dimmed, almost sorrowful, yet steady. "Mpande, hear me. This battle is already lost. Nothing you do here can change its ending. To stay is to fade into memory, bound to a story not your own. And all the while, your true world waits—time slipping away while you wander another's past."

Her words cut deep, sharper than any blade. I felt torn between duty and truth, between the weight of the moment and the call of eternity.

"I… I'll go back," Mpande said, his voice steady, a new calm weaving through him. He turned, letting his gaze drift down toward Earth, expecting familiar landscapes, but what he saw was anything but familiar. Africa sprawled beneath him, yet the continent seemed transformed, reshaped. Other lands appeared where maps he had known marked none, coastlines and rivers twisting like the hand of a painter drunk on possibility. He opened his mouth to ask, but Nkanyezi interrupted before the words formed.

Her eyes shone like the nebulae themselves. "I can't believe I'm meeting my son like this, after hundreds of years since I lived on the Rock," she said with a quiet marvel. "Yes, I am your ancestor, Mpande. We cannot waste time on idle chit-chat."

She extended her hand to him, radiant and strong. "I will always be here, in the sky. "As long as I live, I will be watching and shining a light in the darkest of nights for you and your family for generations to come." Before he could respond, her grip tightened and, with a gentle but firm push, she sent him tumbling into the void.

"Look to the stars, Mpande," she called, her voice echoing in his bones. "You will never be lost."

He laughed, the sound free and reckless, and surrendered to the fall. He was now realizing that the voice that had been guiding him and telling the story was his own.For the first time in a long while, he accepted that control was an illusion — yet gratitude filled him.Grateful to fall and to rise again, to live, and to feel. Darkness enveloped him, and then, with a rush of water and light, he resurfaced from the river portal he had entered before. The cool flow rushed past him, washing the remnants of the vision from his skin.

He swam to the shore, lungs burning and heart racing, only to see Doctor Langa asleep among others by the river, campfires flickering warmly in the distance. Signs of long habitation surrounded him: blankets, tools, and the quiet rhythm of life already in motion.

His gaze caught the only awake figure, and he was struck speechless. Jasmine, her smile radiant, stood in the firelight, warmth spreading from her grin even at a distance. She ran to him, arms wide, and he let himself be swept into her embrace. The people stirred, rose, and songs of praise filled the night.

After what felt like forever, he opened his eyes to find the crowd bowing. Sabelo handed him a robe, and he realized he was already adorned in leopard hide, beads, and gold bracelets which he never dived in with. Though all he wanted was to be with Jasmine, the people had vowed their loyalty, and Doctor Langa's cousin eagerly waited to learn from him. A house had been prepared for him, his family waiting to welcome him back. He was treated like royalty, yet a calm washed over him — a moment to absorb the enormity of it all.

Respectfully, he asked for time alone with his family. This life carried weight he could not yet grasp, and he allowed himself to simply exist within it. At his house, his mother cooked while his siblings played. Their eyes widened, joy breaking into screams as they ran to embrace him. Festivities erupted, laughter blending with the warmth of home. I told them I had found my clan name and would like to use it. Aware of the power that comes with a name we celebrated.

Night fell, and Jasmine guided him to their room, keeping it warm in his absence. His hand brushed her belly, feeling the soft rhythm within — a drumbeat echoing the festivities of the king's court. The joy of fatherhood settled in him like a quiet sunrise. For that moment, it was just them, their world narrowed to love, warmth, and possibility. He envisioned the life he wanted to build, a kingdom for his children, a place rooted in hope and strength.

Jasmine told him how she had discovered her rare magic. A black witch, a kind only once seen in recorded Zulu history, she had come into power in secrecy. Protected kings in history bore witness to the kind of magic she wielded. Her story was as incredible as it was impossible — her Caucasian appearance and her parents, a White Witch and a Wizard, made the tale all the more extraordinary. "Our child," he thought, smiling, "will surely be something else."

Before taking the next steps, Mpande asked to return to the apartment in Hillbrow where he had lived. There was much to prepare: war loomed with a council of witches who would challenge Jasmine's choice to stay and marry into his lineage, as well as battles against those who misused power meant to protect the people. He had to reshape systems, curb greed, and reclaim authority for justice.

Reaching the apartment, he sensed an unusual power within. He urged Jasmine to remain in the car, wary of repeating the elevator incident, and stepped inside alone. Mubanga moved slowly, turning with hands raised, while another man's voice came from the bathroom. Calm, Mpande assessed them, reading their intentions with ease.

"We've been watching over you," Mubanga said, voice steady. "The others and I are tasked with protecting you."

A king's seal was placed in his hand — recognition and authority clear. With it came a folded letter, worn with age but bearing the unmistakable mark of the royal house. Mpande broke the seal carefully, his hands trembling as he read:

'To the one who completes the trial as it was written in prophecy: know this. The wealth of our line, safeguarded and hidden for generations, now belongs to you. It has protected you, and those before you, so that this moment could arrive. With it, you carry not only treasure, but the weight of our hope. Use it to build, to protect, and to lead.'

The words struck him like thunder. This was no mere inheritance—it was legacy, a bridge between past and future.

He left with them for his next stop: the Ndaba Org and being one of the media giants. There, he announced his return as king of a small clan in his inheritance with aspirations in politics, shocking some and thrilling others.

Later, back at his house, he looked up at the night sky, stars scattered like diamonds across black velvet. Jasmine read nearby, calm and radiant. He leapt from the balcony to the garden, approaching a quiet chess game where Mubanga and his friend rose and bowed. He joked about adjusting to their height, took a seat, and accepted a glass of whiskey.

"Let me tell you about the Zulu Hundred, my king," Mubanga began, eyes gleaming with the promise of stories and lessons to come.

Mpande leaned back, the stars above him shining brighter than ever. For the first time in his life, he felt ready — ready for love, for family, for leadership, and for the battles yet to come

---

The End... or so it seems.

And in the silence of the stars, Nkhanyezi's voice lingered:

"First shall come the time of the *White Witches*,
when the hidden ones rise, and truth wears a cloak of shadow.

Then shall follow the *Counsel of Witches*,
where power gathers in secret, binding fate in whispered oaths.

And last, the world shall know of the *Zulu Hundred*,
warriors bound in blood and fire,
who march with kings and reshape the dawn."

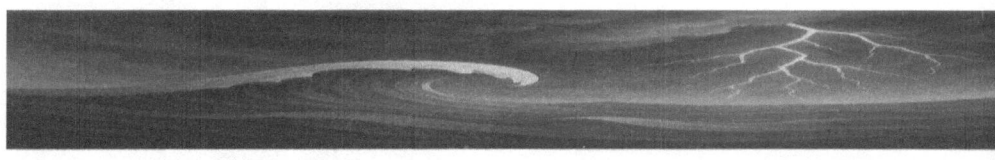

The night had weight, like it had been holding its breath with
him. The fire was down to its last embers, smoke curling into
the dark. He sat there with the silence pressing in, aware of how
far he had come, but also how much further there was still to
go.

The visions didn't fade. They stayed with him—face, places,
battles still waiting. The ancestors had whispered, but whispers
were never the end. They were beginnings. He knew now that
this path was not just about survival or proving himself. It was
about building something greater, something that stretched
beyond his own breath. He felt both heavy and light at once.
Heavy with the weight of all that had happened, the scars he

carried, the choices made. Light because for the first time he wasn't just drifting. The road wasn't clear, but it was his.

The fire cracked once, like a final word. He stood, looking out into the dark, no longer afraid of it. This was not the end. It was only the first telling of a much larger story. A story that would not end here, but only pause, waiting for the next chapter.

About the Author

Sandile Mchunu was born and raised in South Africa. A lover of hip-hop, history, and stories that carry more than just words, he sees writing as both healing and rebellion. *Abelumbi – The White Witches* is his first book, the opening chapter of a saga that blends folklore, imagination, and the battles of the spirit.

This is only the beginning of the Abelumbi saga:

- **Abelumbi – The White Witches** *(Book One, the story you've just read)*
- **Abelumbi – Counsel of Witches** *(Book Two)*
- **Abelumbi and The Zulu 100** *(Book Three)*

The White Witches was only the spark… the Counsel awaits, and the Zulu 100 are rising.